FOAL

CARRYING HIS
SCANDALOUS HEIR

CARRYING HIS
SCANDALOUS HEIR

JULIA JAMES

MILLS & BOON

First published in Great Britain 2017
by Mills & Boon, an imprint of HarperCollins*Publishers*
1 London Bridge Street, London, SE1 9GF

Large Print edition 2018

© 2017 Julia James

ISBN: 978-0-263-07358-4

MIX
Paper from
responsible sources
FSC C007454

This book is produced from independently certified
FSC™ paper to ensure responsible forest management.
For more information visit www.harpercollins.co.uk/green.

Printed and bound in Great Britain
by CPI Group (UK) Ltd, Croydon, CR0 4YY

For Kathryn—thank you for all your hard work!

CHAPTER ONE

CARLA LOOKED AT her watch for the umpteenth time, glancing out across the crowded restaurant towards the entrance. Where *was* he? Anxiety bit at her, and an emotion more powerful than that—one she had never felt before. Had never thought to feel about the man she was waiting for.

She had thought only to feel what she had felt the first time she had set eyes on him. And she so desperately wanted to set eyes on him again now—walking in, striding with his effortlessly assured gait, tall and commanding, with that in-built assumption that he could go wherever he liked, that there would always be a place for him, that people would move aside to let him through, that no one would ever dream of turning him down or saying no to him—not about anything at all.

She had not turned him down. She had denied

him nothing—granted him everything. Everything he'd ever wanted of her…

Memory, hot and fervid, scorched within her. From the very first moment those hooded night-dark eyes had rested on her, assessing her, desiring her, she had been lost. Utterly lost! She had yielded to him with the absolute conviction that he was the only man who could ever have such an impact on her. That moment was imprinted on her—on her memory, on her suddenly heating body…on her heart.

Memory scorched again now, burning through her veins…

The art gallery was crowded with Rome's wealthy, fashionable set, and champagne and canapés were circling as Carla threaded her way among them, murmuring words of greeting here and there.

Reaching for a glass of gently foaming champagne, Carla knew that she herself could be counted as one of them. Oh, not by birth or breeding, but as the stepdaughter of multi-millionaire Guido Viscari she could move in circles such as these and hold her own and look the part.

Her cocktail dress in a deep blue raw silk had come from one of the currently favoured fashion houses, and it hugged a figure that easily passed muster amongst all the couture-clad females there. Her face, too, as she well knew, also passed muster. Her features veered towards the dramatic, with eyes that could flash with fire and full lips that gave a hint of inner sensuousness.

It was a face that drew male eyes, and she could sense them now—especially since she was there on her own. Unlike many of the other guests, she had a genuine reason for attending this private viewing other than simply being there to while away an hour or so before dining.

But she'd long got used to the constant perusal that Italian men habitually bestowed upon females. It had shocked and discomfited her ten years ago, when she'd been a raw English teenager new to Italian life, but since then she'd grown inured to it. Now she hardly ever noticed the looks that came her way.

Except— She stilled suddenly, the champagne glass halfway to her lips. *Someone was looking at her.* Someone whose gaze she could feel on her like a physical touch. Her eyes shifted their line of sight. Someone who was making her the centre of his observations.

And then, as her gaze moved, she saw him.

He'd just come into the gallery. The receptionist at the welcome desk was still smiling up at him, but he was ignoring her, instead glancing out across the room. Carla felt a little thrill go through her, as though somewhere deep inside her a seismic shock were taking place, and she noticed his gaze was focussing on *her*.

She felt her breath catch, seize in her throat. She felt a sudden flush of heat go through her. For the man making her the object of his scrutiny was the most devastating male she had ever seen.

He was tall, powerfully built with broad shoulders, his features strong…compelling. With a blade of a nose, night-dark hair, night-dark eyes, and a mobile mouth with a twist to it that did strange things to her.

Unknown things…

Things she had never experienced before.

The flush of heat in her body intensified. She felt pinned—as though movement were impossible, as though she had just been caught in a noose—captured.

Captivated.

For how long he went on subjecting her to that measuring, assessing scrutiny she could not tell—knew only that it seemed to be timeless.

She felt her lungs grow parched of oxygen... Then, suddenly, she was released. Someone had come up to him—another man, greeting him effusively—and his eyes relinquished hers, his face turning away from her.

She took a lungful of air, feeling shaken.

What had just happened?

The question seared within her...and burned. How could a single glance do that to her? Have such an effect on her?

Jerkily, she took a mouthful of champagne, needing its chill to cool the heat flushing through her. She stepped away, averting her body, making herself do what she had come there to do— study the portraits that were the subject of the exhibition.

Her eyes lifted to the one opposite her.

And as they did so another shock went through

her. She was staring—yet again—into a pair of night-dark eyes. The same eyes…the *very* same.

Night-dark, hooded, sensuous…

That little thrill went through her again, that flush of heat moved in her body. The portrait's eyes seemed to be subjecting her to the same kind of measuring scrutiny that the man by the door had focussed on her.

She tore her eyes away from the face that looked out at her from the portrait. Moved them down to the brass plate at the side of the frame. She hardly needed to read it—she knew perfectly well who the artist was.

Andrea Luciezo, who, along with Titian, was one of the great masters of the High Renaissance. His ability to capture the essence of those who had sat for him—the rich, the powerful, the men who had controlled the Italy of the sixteenth century, the women who had adorned them—had brought them vividly, vibrantly, to life. Luciezo—whose dark, glowing oils, lustrous and lambent, infused each subject with a richly potent glamour.

Her eyes went from the name of the artist to

that of his subject. She gave a slow, accepting nod. *Yes, of course.*

Her gaze went back to the man in the portrait. He looked out at all those who gazed at him with dark, hooded, assessing eyes. She looked at the powerful features, the raven hair, worn long to the nape of the strong neck, his jaw bearded in the fashion of the time, yet leaving unhidden the sensuous line of his mouth, the unbearably rich velvet of his black doublet, the stark pleated white of his deep collar, the glint of precious gold at his broad, powerful chest.

He was a man whom the artist knew considered his own worth high, whose portrait told all who gazed upon it that here was no ordinary mortal, cut from the common herd. Arrogance was in that hooded gaze, in the angle of his head, the set of his shoulders. He was a man for whom the world would do his bidding—whatever he bade them do...

A voice spoke behind her. Deep, resonant. With a timbre to it that set off yet again that low, internal seismic tremor.

'So,' he said, as she stood immobile in front of

the portrait, 'what do you think of my ancestor, Count Alessandro?'

She turned, lifted her face, let her eyes meet the living version of the dark, hooded gaze that had transfixed her across the centuries—the living version that had transfixed her only moments ago and was now transfixing her again.

Cesare di Mondave, Conte di Mantegna.

The owner of this priceless Luciezo portrait of his ancestor, and of vast wealth besides. A man whose reputation went before him—a reputation for living in the same fashion as his illustrious forebears: as if the whole world belonged to him. To whom no one would say no—and to whom any woman upon whom he looked with favour would want to say only one thing.

Yes.

And as Carla met his gaze, felt its impact, its power and potency, she knew with a hollow sense of fatalism that it was the only word *she* would ever want to use.

'Well?'

The deep voice came again and Carla realised that she needed to speak—had been commanded to answer him. For this was a man who was obeyed.

But she would not obey immediately. She would defy him in that, at least.

Deliberately she looked back at the Luciezo, making him wait. 'A man of his time,' she answered finally.

As you are not a man of your time.

The words formed in her head silently, powerfully. No, the current Conte di Mantegna was *not* a man of the twenty-first century! She could see it in every austere line of his body. He carried his own ancient ancestry in the unconscious lift of his chin at her reply, in his dark brows drawing together.

'What do you mean by that?'

Again, the question demanded an immediate answer.

Carla looked back at the portrait, gathering her reasons for the reply she had made him.

'His hand is on the pommel of his sword,' she essayed. 'He will slay any man who offers him insult. He subjects himself to the scrutiny of one who can never be his equal, however much genius Luciezo possesses, simply in order that his illustrious image can be displayed. His arrogance is in every line, every stroke of the brush.'

She turned back to the man who had commanded her to speak. Her answer had displeased him, as she had known it would.

There was a dark flash in his eyes, as he riposted, 'You mistake arrogance for pride. Pride not in himself but in his family, his lineage, his honour. An honour he would defend with his life, with his sword, —that he *must* defend because he has no choice but to do so. The artist's scrutiny is to be endured because he must be ever mindful of what he owes his house—which is to protect it and preserve it. His portrait will be his persona in his own absence—it will persist for posterity when he himself is dust.'

The night-dark eyes went to those in the portrait. As if, Carla thought, the two men were communing with each other.

Her brow furrowed for an instant. How strange to think that a man of the present could look into the eyes of his own ancestor... That, in itself, made *il Conte* entirely different from all those who—like herself—were simply cut from the common herd of humanity…who had no knowledge of their ancestors from so many centuries ago.

Her expression changed, becoming drawn for a moment. She didn't even know of her own more immediate forebears. Her father was little more than a name to her—a name reluctantly bestowed upon her when her mother's pregnancy had required that he marry her, only for him to be killed in a car crash when she was a small child. His widow had been unwelcome to her in-laws, and Carla had been raised by her mother alone until her remarriage to Guido Viscari when Carla was a young teenager.

I know more about my stepfather's family than I do about my own father's!

To a man like *il Conte* that very ignorance about her paternal forebears must seem incomprehensible, for he would know the identity of every one of his entire collection of ancestors for centuries—each of them doubtless from families as aristocratic as his own.

With such a heritage she could not be surprised by his immediate retort. Yet she had one of her own.

'Then it is entirely to the credit of Luciezo's mastery that he can convey all that with his portrait,' she replied, making her voice even. 'Without his genius to record it your ancestor *is* merely dust.'

There was defiance in her voice—and an open assertion that, however many heraldic quarterings the illustrious Conte di Mantegna was possessed of, none could compare with the incomparable genius of a great master such as Luciezo.

That dark flash came again in the depths of the Conte's eyes. 'Will we not all be dust in years to come?' he murmured. 'But until that time comes...'

Something changed in his voice—something that suddenly made the heat flush in her blood once more, as it had done when she had realised his gaze was upon her.

'Should we not *carpe diem*?'

'Seize the day?' Carla heard her voice answering. But inside her head she was registering that sudden change in the Count's voice, the smoothing of that low timbre. She could see, now, the change in his eyes. He was looking at her. Approving of what he saw. Sending that flush of heat through her again.

'Or, indeed, seize the evening,' he murmured again, with the slightest husk in his voice.

And now there was no mistaking the message in his voice. None at all. Those dark, long-lashed hooded eyes were resting on her, and the message in them was as old as time.

She pleased him. Her appearance, at any rate, even if her words did not. But their exchange had merely been the mechanism by which he had approached her—had given him the opening he desired, by which he would obtain the end he sought.

The end he now stated openly.

'Have dinner with me tonight.'

It was as simple as that. As straightforward. His dark, expressive eyes were resting on her, and Carla felt their impact—knew their message.

Knew what reply she should make to this power-ful, sensual man, who was displaying every obvious sign of his intent.

Her habit had always been to say no—the few relationships she'd had over the years had never been with Italians, nor conducted in Rome under the avidly speculative glare of the circles in which she moved. And never had she fancied herself to be deeply emotionally involved. It had been only friendship and compatibility that attracted her—no more than that. It was safer that way. Safer than yielding to any overriding sensual attraction that might ignite a passion that would be hard to quench.

After all, no one knew better than she what *that* might lead to. Hadn't it happened to her own mother? Falling for a man who, when he'd been faced with unintended pregnancy, had not wished to commit to her?

Although his father had cracked the financial whip and forced a marriage, there had been no happy ending. Her father had chafed at marriage, chafed at fatherhood—and had been on the point of leaving her mother when he was killed. Was it any wonder, Carla asked herself, that she was wary of making such a mistake herself?

So, for every reason of good sense, there was only one reply for her to make to this arrogant, sensual man who possessed the power to disturb her senses.

Yet she could not say the words. Could only find the means to give a slight, fleeting, demurring half-smile, and a self-protective sweeping down of her eyelashes to hide the all too revealing response in her eyes as she made an evasive reply.

'So…have you loaned any other paintings to the exhibition?' she asked.

Her voice sounded abrupt, even breathless, but she did not care. She met his gaze head-on, keeping hers quite limpid, though the effort was great—the more so since in his eyes was a look of knowingness that told her he had understood immediately why she had not answered him.

But to her relief he followed her diversion.

'Indeed,' he murmured, still with that semi-amused look in his eyes that was so disturbing to her. 'The Luciezo is, in fact, part of a triptych.

The other two portraits are on display across the gallery.'

There was a discernible tinge of annoyance in his voice at the curator's decision as he indicated across the width of the gallery, towards an alcove in which Carla could make out two portraits.

'Shall we?'

The cool voice held assumption, and Carla found herself being guided forward. He halted, lifting his hand to the portraits they were now in front of.

'What do you make of them?'

Carla's trained eyes went to the portraits, immediately seeing the skill and artistry in them, seeing in them all the hallmarks of a master. Her eyes narrowed very slightly. But not Luciezo.

'Caradino?' she ventured.

She felt rather than saw the glance the Count threw at her. Surprise—and approval.

'Caradino,' he confirmed. He paused. 'Many attribute his few surviving works to Luciezo.'

She gave a slight shake of her head. 'No,' she said. 'There is a discernible difference.'

Her eyes ran over the portraits, taking in the

brushwork, the lighting, the shadows. Her gaze went from appraising the technicalities of the portraits to the subjects themselves. And then, for the first time, her eyes widened as her gaze rested on their faces.

So unalike. So very, *very* unalike.

One so fair and pale. A married woman, clearly, as illustrated by the tokens in the painting—her pearl earring, the sprig of myrtle in her lap, the dish of quinces on the little table at her side—and yet there was about her, Carla could see, an air almost of virginity…as if with different garments and accoutrements she might have modelled for a painting of the Virgin Mary.

A crucifix was in her hands, glinting between her long, pale fingers. Carla looked at the woman's eyes.

Sadness. As if, like the Virgin Mary, she had in her gaze a foretelling of the great sorrows that were to come.

She pulled her gaze away. Let it rest on the other woman's face.

Another young woman. In this portrait the subject's hair was a lush chestnut-brown, lavishly unbound and snaking down over one bare shoulder. Her gown was a sumptuous red, not a celestial blue, and cut low across her generous bosom to reveal an expansive amount of soft, creamy skin. She held red roses in her hands, rubies gleamed at her throat and on her fingers, and her hands rested on her abdomen—its slight swell discreet, but undeniable.

Carla drew her eyes away from the telltale curve of the young woman's figure, moved them back up to scrutinise her face. Beautiful, in a sensuous way, framed by her rich tresses, her cheeks flushed, lips full and with a sensual cast to them. Carla's eyes went to the woman's eyes and held them for a long moment—held the unseeing gaze that looked out over the centuries between the two of them.

'Who *are* they?'

Her own voice cut short her perusal, and she drew her gaze away to look back at *il Conte*, standing at her side.

'Can you not tell?' he asked. He glanced back to the portrait of his ancestor, across the room, then back to Carla. 'His wife—and his mistress.

He had them painted at the same time, by the same hand. Caradino stayed at my *castello* and painted them both—one after the other.'

Carla's face stilled. 'How nice for them,' she said drily. 'It seems your ancestor kept his mistress…handy.'

But the Count did not rise to her sardonic comment. 'It was quite normal in those times. Nothing exceptional. Both women knew and understood the situation.'

Carla's lips pressed together. 'Knowing and understanding are not the same thing as tolerating and agreeing,' she riposted.

The dark, hooded eyes were veiled. 'Women had no power in those times. And after all,' he went on, 'my ancestor's mistress was *very* lavishly looked after.'

'She's carrying his child,' Carla retorted.

She could feel an emotion rising up in her—one she did not want to feel, but it was coming all the same.

'An excellent way to secure the Count's protection,' agreed Cesare. 'I believe they had several children, over the years. He was very faithful to her, you know. Surprisingly so for the times.'

Automatically Carla's eyes went not to the mistress of the former Count but to his wife. No sign of fertility there—and in the eyes only that haunting sadness.

Thoughts ran through her head, unstoppable.

How did she feel? How did she cope? Knowing her husband was having children, openly, with his mistress? Yet presumably she, too, must have had an heir, at least, or the line would have died out—which it obviously hasn't?

'But enough of my ancestors—have you seen the other paintings displayed here yet?'

The voice of the man at her side drew her back to the present. She turned towards him. Saw him with fresh eyes, it seemed. Her gaze went past him to the portrait of Count Alessandro, who had been so unconcerned as to have his wife and mistress painted simultaneously.

A shaft of female indignation went through her, as she brought her gaze back to the current Count.

'Not all of them yet, no,' she said. She made

her voice purposeful. 'And I really must. I have fifteen hundred words to write up about the exhibition.'

She named the arts magazine she wrote for, as if she was aware that by stressing her professional interest she would diminish her personal one.

'And I must do my duty by all the paintings here!'

She spoke lightly but deliberately. She smiled. An equally deliberate smile. One that completely ignored the question he had asked her only a few minutes ago, making no reference to it.

'Thank you so much, Signor il Conte, for showing me these fascinating portraits, and for giving me such insight into them. It's always enhancing to learn the origins and the circumstances of a portrait's creation—it brings it so to life! And especially since the artist Caradino is so seldom exhibited.'

She smiled again—the same social smile—signalling closure. For closure, surely, was essential. Anything else would be...

Her mind veered away, not wanting to think

of the path she had not taken. The yielding she had not made.

Instead she gave the slightest nod of her head in parting and walked away. Her high heels clicked on the parquet flooring and as she walked she was intensely conscious of his following gaze, of how her shapely figure was outlined by the vivid tailored dress she was wearing. Intensely conscious of the urge overwhelming her to get away. Just…*away*.

As she walked, she sipped at her champagne again. She felt the need of it. Her colour was heightened, she knew—knew it from the hectic beating of her heart.

He desires me—the Conte di Mantegna has looked at me and found me pleasing to him…

Into her head sprang an image, immediate and vivid, conjured out of her ready imagination. That woman in the portrait—the brunette—working, perhaps, in her father's shop, or sweeping floors, or even toiling out in the fields in sixteenth-century Italy… *Il Conte* passing by, seeing her, liking her beauty, taking a fancy to her. Finding her pleasing to him. Lifting her with one beckoning of his lordly, aristocratic hand out of her hard, poverty-stricken life to dress her in a silk gown and place roses in her hands and jewels around her throat, and take her to his bed...

She felt the pull of it—the allure. Had to force herself to remember all that would have gone with it. The price that woman would have paid.

To know that her place in his life was only ever to be his inamorata—*never to aspire to be his wife.*

And as for the Count—oh, he would have had everything he wanted. His pale, subservient wife—his compliant, obliging mistress.

Having it all.

She dragged her mind away, making herself inspect the other paintings, consult her catalogue, interview the exhibition's curator, and then get a few words from the gallery's director, who greeted her warmly, both in her professional capacity and as the stepdaughter of the late chairman of a global hotel chain—a generous patron of the arts himself.

It had been her stepfather who'd first noticed her interest in art as a teenager, and it was thanks to him that she'd studied history of art at prestigious universities both in England and Italy. He'd encouraged her in her journalistic career. It was a career she found immensely satisfying, and she knew herself to be extremely fortunate in it.

Now, with all her notes taken, she was ready to leave. She'd spend the evening going through them, drawing up the article she would write.

As she made her farewells she found herself glancing around. She knew who it was she was trying to glimpse. And knew why she should not be. Cesare di Mondave was far too disturbing to her peace of mind to allow herself to have anything more to do with him.

He was not to be seen anyway, and she told herself she was glad. Relieved. Because to further her acquaintance with Cesare di Mondave would *not* be good sense at all.

Involuntarily her eyes went to the portrait of his ancestor—Count Alessandro, regarding the world in all his High Renaissance splendour, his dark gaze compelling, arrogant. In her mind's eye she saw his wife and his mistress. Two women, rivals for ever, their destinies yoked to the man who had commissioned their portraits.

Had they both loved him? Or neither?

The question hovered in her head, its answer long consumed by the centuries that had passed. All she could know, with a kind of ironic certainty, was that it would not be wise for *any* woman to have anything to do with the man in whose veins ran the blood of Luciezo's Count Alessandro.

It didn't matter that his descendant could have an impact on her that she had never encountered before. That his dark lidded eyes could raise her pulse in an instant…that her eyes had wanted only to cling helplessly, hopelessly, to his sculpted, powerful features, that her hand had yearned to reach towards him, graze the tanned skin of his jaw, brush the sensual swell of his mouth… It didn't matter at all.

Because letting herself get embroiled with the

arrogant, oh-so-aristocratic Count of Mantegna would be folly indeed!

She was not, and never would be, like the lush beauty in the Caradino portrait, haplessly dependent upon the Count's continuing desire for her, fearing its demise. Her lips thinned slightly. Nor could she ever be like the woman in the other portrait—oh, she might move in Roman high society, but the Viscaris were hoteliers: rich, but with no trace of aristocratic blood. Carla knew without flinching that when *il Conte* chose a wife, it would be a woman from his own background, with an ancestry to match his.

I would be nothing more than an...an interlude for him.

She walked out onto the pavement and into the warm evening air of Rome in late summer. A low, lean, open-topped car was hovering at the kerb, blatantly ignoring the road signs forbidding such parking. Its powerful engine was throbbing with a throaty husk, its scarlet paintwork was gleaming, and the rearing stallion on the long bonnet caught the light, glinting gold like the crested signet ring on the hand curved around the wheel.

The man at the wheel turned his head. Let his dark, lidded gaze rest on Carla.

'What kept you?' asked Cesare di Mondave, Conte di Mantegna.

CHAPTER TWO

CESARE'S HAND RESTED on the leather curve of the steering wheel. Impatience was humming in him. He appreciated that she had a job to do—this woman his eyes had lit upon, drawn without conscious intent to her dramatic beauty, her voluptuous figure, the extraordinarily dark blue eyes that had a hint of violet in them—but for all that he did not care to be kept waiting.

He'd known who she was before he'd made the decision to approach her—he'd seen her about previously in society, even though the aristocratic circles *he* moved in overlapped only loosely with those of the Viscaris. The Viscaris were, to him, 'new money'—it was a mere handful of generations since the global hotel group that bore the family name had been founded at the end of the nineteenth century. They were newcomers compared to the immense antiquity of *his* family—

and Cesare felt the weight of that antiquity upon him each and every day.

It was a weight that both upheld him and imposed upon him responsibilities to his ancestry that others could not understand. A duty that reached far back into the Middle Ages, stretching across all his estates from the high Apennine lands leased as a national park, to forests and vineyards, agricultural land and olive groves, and across all his many properties. Every *palazzo* was a historic monument, including the magnificent baroque Palazzo Mantegna here in Rome, now on loan to the nation and housing a museum of antiquities. And all those estates and properties came with tenants and employees whose livelihood he guaranteed—just as his ancestors had.

Yet at the heart of it all was the ancient Castello Mantegna, the heart of his patrimony. Within its mighty walls, built to withstand medieval warfare, he had spent his childhood, roaming the forests and pasturelands that one day would be his.

Was that something anyone not born to such a heritage could truly understand? The weight of inheritance upon him?

Or did they merely see *il Conte*—a wealthy, titled man who moved in the uppermost echelons of society, with a cachet that many would only envy? And which women would eagerly seek to bask in…

His dark eyes glinted. There had been no such eagerness in Carla Charteris, though he'd made clear his interest in her. He was glad of it—but not deterred by it. For his long experience of woman had told him immediately that the first flare of her violet-hued eyes as he'd addressed her had showed that she was responsive to him. That was all he'd needed to know—their barbed exchange thereafter had merely confirmed it. All that was required now was for her to acknowledge it.

He leant across to open the passenger side door. *'Prego,'* he invited in a pleasant voice.

He'd surprised her—he could tell. Had she really believed that walking away from him would discourage him?

He went on in a dry voice, 'It would gratify me if you complied without delay, for the traffic warden over there—' he nodded carelessly along the street to where such an individual had recently turned the corner '—would so very much enjoy booking me.' He gave a brief sigh. 'I find that officials take particular pleasure in exercising their petty authority when their target is driving a car like this one.'

He smiled. He could see the conflict in her eyes—in those amazingly dark violet-blue eyes of hers—but above all he could see that same flare of awareness, of desire, which had been in them when he'd first approached her. That told him all he needed to know.

His expression changed again. *'Carpe diem,'* he said softly. His eyes held hers. Tellingly, un-ambiguously. 'Let us seize all that we may have of this fleeting life,' he murmured, 'before we are dust ourselves.'

His casual reference to her own comment in front of the Luciezo was accompanied by an ex-aggerated gesture of his hand as he again indi-cated the seat beside him.

His lashes dipped over his eyes. 'What is so difficult,' he murmured, 'about accepting an in-vitation to dinner?' His gaze lifted to hers again, and in his eyes was everything that was not in his words.

Carla, her expression immediately urgently schooled, stopped in her tracks on the pavement, felt again that incredible frisson go through her whole body—that shimmer of glittering aware-ness of the physical impact he made on her.

All around her the city of Rome buzzed with its familiar vitality. The warmth of the early evening enveloped her, and she could hear the noise of the traffic, the buzz of endless Vespas scooting past. The pavement was hot beneath the thin soles of her high heels. While in front of her, in that out-rageously expensive car—as exclusive and pres-tigious as its driver so undoubtedly considered himself to be—the oh-so-aristocratic Conte in-vited her to join him.

As she had before, in the gallery, she felt the overwhelming impact of the man. Felt even more powerfully the impulse within her to give him the answer that he was waiting for.

Thoughts—fragmented, incoherent—raced through her.

What is happening to me? Why now—why this

man of all men? This arrogant, lordly man who is scooping me up as if I were no more than that woman in the portrait—scooping me up to serve his pleasure...

Yet it would be for *her* pleasure too—she knew that with every shimmer in her body as she stood, poised on the pavement, feeling the weight of his lidded gaze upon her. That was the devil of it— that was the allure. That was the reason, Carla knew with a kind of sinking in her heart, that was keeping her here, hovering, just as he was keeping that monstrous, powerful car of his hovering, its power leashed, but ready to be let forth.

His words, mocking her, echoed in her head. *'What is so difficult about accepting an invitation to dinner?'*

His voice—deep, amused—cut across her tormented cogitations. 'You really will need to decide swiftly—the warden is nearly upon us.'

The uniformed official was, indeed, closing fast. But Carla's eyes only sparked deep blue. 'And you couldn't *possibly* afford the fine, could you?' she retorted.

'Alas, it is a question of my pride,' Cesare murmured, the glint in his eye accentuated. 'It would never do for *il Conte* to put himself in the power of a petty bureaucrat...'

Was he mocking himself? Carla had the suspicion he was not...

For a moment longer every objection she had made when he'd first invited her to dinner flared like phosphorus in her head. Every reason why she should give exactly the same kind of answer as she had then—evasive, avoiding the invitation—then walk briskly away, back to the comfortable, predictable evening she'd planned for herself in her own apartment. Making herself dinner, going through her notes in preparation for writing her article. An evening that had nothing, *nothing* to do with the man now waiting for her answer...

And yet—

Her own thought replayed itself in her head. *How dangerous might it be to light a passion that could not be quenched?*

But other thoughts pushed their way into her head. Thoughts she did not want to silence. Could not silence… *Desire and passion will burn themselves out! They cannot last for ever.*

Neither desire nor passion was love.

Yet both were powerful—alluring—speaking to her of what might be between them.

Passion and desire.

The same tremor went through her, the same flush in her skin as when he had first made his desire for her plain, calling from her an answering awareness. No other man had ever drawn from her such an overpowering response.

For a second longer she hesitated, hung between two opposing instincts.

To resist that response—or to yield to it.

The dark, lidded eyes rested on her—holding hers.

With a sudden impulse, impelling her way below the level of conscious decision, she felt her muscles move as if of their own volition. She got into the car, slamming the door shut.

Instantly, as if preventing her from rescinding her decision as much as avoiding the attentions of the parking official, Cesare opened the throttle, pulled the car away from the kerb—and Carla reached for her seat belt, consciousness rushing back upon her in all its impact.

Oh, dear God, what the *hell* had she just done?

I got into his damn car just to save his damn aristocratic pride! So he wouldn't have to endure the ignominy of getting a parking ticket! How insane is that?

Completely insane. As insane as letting Cesare di Mondave drive off with her like this—the lordly *signor* scooping up the peasant girl.

Her chin lifted. Well, she was no peasant girl! She was no poor, hapless female like the one in the portrait, trapped within the punishing limitations of her time in history. No, if she went along with what this impossible, arrogant man had in mind for her—*if*, she emphasised mentally to herself—then it would be what *she* wanted too! Her free and deliberate choice to enjoy the enticing interlude he clearly had planned.

But would she make that choice? That was the only question that mattered now. Whether to do what every ounce of her good sense was telling her she should not do—and what every heat-flushed cell in her body was urging her to do. To resist it—or yield to it. She turned her head towards him, drawn by that same impetuous urge to let her eyes feast on him. He was focussing only on the appalling evening traffic in Rome, which, she allowed, *did* need total focus. She let him concentrate, let herself enjoy the rush that came simply from looking at his profile.

Sweet heaven, but it was impossible not to gaze at him! A modern version of that Luciezo portrait, updated for the twenty-first century. Indelibly graced with features that made her eyes cling to him, from the strong blade of his nose to the chiselled line of his jaw, the sensual curve of his mouth. She felt her hands clench over her bag. Weakness drenched her body. What she was doing was insane—and yet she was doing it.

She felt her pulse leap, and a heady sense of excitement filled her. A searing knowledge of her own commitment. Far too late now to change her mind.

And she did not want to—that was the crux of it. Oh, the lordly Count might have scooped her up just as arrogantly as his ancestor had scooped up the peasant girl who would become his mistress, but it had been *her* choice to let herself be so scooped.

Rebelliousness soared within her—a sense of recklessness and adventure.

I don't care if this is folly! All I know is that from the moment he looked at me I wanted him more than I have ever wanted any man—and I will not deny that desire. I will fulfil it...

Fulfil it with all the ardour in her body, every tremor in her limbs. It was folly—reckless folly—but she would ignite that passion and burn it to the core.

'Take the next left here,' Carla said, indicating the narrow road in the Centro Storico that led down to her apartment, part of an eighteenth-century house. It was a quiet haven for her to write in, and to be well away not just from the buzz of the city but also from the tensions running across the Viscari clan.

Her mother, she knew, would have preferred her to stay on in Guido Viscari's opulent villa, but thanks to her stepfather's generosity in his will Carla had been able to buy her own small but beautiful apartment, taking intense pleasure in decorating it and furnishing it in an elegant but comfortable and very personal style.

However, her thoughts now were neither on the ongoing tensions in the Viscari clan nor on her apartment. There was only one dominating, all-encompassing consciousness in her head...

Cesare.

Cesare—with whom she had just dined, with whom she had conducted, she knew, a conversation that had taken place at two levels. One had seen him being the perfect escort, the perfect dinner companion, conversing with her about her job, about the arts, about the Italian landscape—of which he owned a significant proportion—and about any other such topics that two people making each other's acquaintance might choose to converse about.

He'd asked her a little about herself—neither too little to be indifferent, nor too much to be intrusive. He'd known who she was, but she was not surprised—she'd known who *he* was, though they'd never chanced to meet before.

But there'd been another conversation taking

place as they'd sat there over a lingering dinner in the small, ferociously exclusive restaurant Cesare had taken her to—where he had immediately been given the best table in the house, and where they had been waited on attentively, discreetly, unobtrusively but with absolute expertise.

He had nodded at one or two other patrons, and her presence had caused the lift of an eyebrow from one group of women, and a penetrating glance, but no more than that. She had been acquainted with no one there, and was glad of it. Glad there had been no one she knew to witness the second level of the conversation taking place between herself and Cesare di Mondave, Conte di Mantegna.

The conversation that had taken place powerfully, silently and seductively—oh-so-seductively—between him and her, with every exchange of glances, every half-smile, every sensual curve of his mouth, every lift of his hand with those long, aristocratic fingers.

The light had reflected off the gold of his signet ring, impressed with his family crest—the same lion couchant that his ancestor had displayed on his own ring in the Luciezo portrait—and Carla had found herself wondering if it could be the very same ring.

Eventually Cesare's hand had crushed the white damask napkin and dropped it on the table to signal the end of their meal, and they'd got to their feet and made their way towards the exit.

Nothing so crude as a bill had been offered by the maître d'—nothing more than a respectful inclination of the head at their departure, a gracious murmur of appreciation from the Count, a smile of thanks from herself as they left, stepping out onto the pavement, where his car had been waiting for them.

Now, as they drew up at the kerb by her apartment, he cut the engine and turned and looked at her, an enigmatic expression visible in the dim street light.

Her consciousness of his raw physical presence seared in her again. She smiled at him. 'Thank you,' she said, 'for a lovely evening.' Her voice was bright, and oh-so-civil.

She realised she'd spoken in English. They'd gone in and out of Italian and English all evening, for the Count's English was as fluent as her Italian had become in the ten years she'd lived in Rome, though surely no Englishman could make his native language as seductive, as sensual as an Italian male could make it sound?

But English was the right language for this moment. Crisp, bright and utterly unseductive. The polite, anodyne description of something that had been so much more. She reached out her hand for the door release, her body still turned towards him.

A smile curved his mouth, long lashes dropping over his lidded eyes. 'Indeed,' he agreed.

She could hear the amusement in his voice, feel it catch at her, making her breathless, her pulse quicken.

'And after such a *"lovely evening"*…' his amusement was deeper now, his accented English doing even more to make her breathless '…there is only one way to end it, no?'

For an instant he held her gaze in the dim light, daring her to accept, to concede, to do what he wanted her to do—what he'd wanted of her from the first moment he'd set eyes on her.

'Like this,' he said.

His hand stretched out, long fingers tilting up her face to his as his mouth lowered to hers. Slowly, sensuously, savouring. With skill, with expertise, with a lifetime of experience in how to let his lips glide over hers, his mouth to open hers to his, to taste the sweetness within. As soft, as sensual as silk velvet.

She drowned in it. A thousand nerve endings fired as he made free with her mouth, his long fingers still holding her. And when he had done he released her, drew back his hand, let it curve around the driving wheel.

He smiled. *'Buone notte,'* he said softly.

For a moment—just a moment—she was motionless, as if all the shimmering pleasure he'd aroused in her with only a single kiss had made it impossible for her to move. She could do nothing except meet that amused, lidded gaze resting on her like a tangible pressure.

Then, with a little jolt, she pushed open the car door. Swallowed. In a daze she got out, fumbled for her keys, found them and shakily inserted them into the lock of the outer door of her apartment building. Then she made herself turn to look back at him. Bade him goodnight in a voice that was no longer bright and crisp.

He said nothing, merely inclining his head as she turned away, let herself into the cobbled inner courtyard, shut the heavy outer door behind her.

She heard the throaty growl of his car as he moved off. On shaky legs she went up to her apartment, and only when inside its sanctuary did she feel able to breathe again.

Cesare strolled to the window of his Rome apartment and gazed unseeing out over the familiar roofline. The large plate glass window of the modern designed space was glaringly different from the richly historical interiors of his other properties, and it gave a wide view over the city even at this midnight hour. He did not step out onto the large adjoining balcony; instead he merely continued to stand, hands thrust into his trouser pockets, legs slightly astride.

Was he being wise? That was the question that was imposing itself upon him. Was it wise to pursue what had been, after all, only the impulse of a moment—following through on a momentary glimpse of the woman who had caught his eye? Following through sufficiently to decide that it was worth spending an evening of his life in her company. Worth considering, as he was now considering, whether to pursue a liaison with her.

There were many reasons to do so. Uppermost, of course, was the intensity of his physical response to her. Unconsciously he shifted position restlessly, his body aware that a single kiss had only whetted the appetite that he could feel coursing through his blood. It was an intensity that had, he acknowledged, taken him by surprise. But was that reason enough to do what he knew his body wanted him to do?

Before he could answer, he knew from long experience that there was another question he must answer first.

Will she understand the terms of our liaison?

The terms that governed his life just as they'd governed all who had borne his ancient name and title. Had been hammered into him by his own dictatorial father who'd constantly impressed upon him his heritage, and yet who'd regarded him as favouring too much the mother whose outward serenity Cesare was sure had concealed an unvoiced regret.

Her husband had objected to her having any interests outside her responsibilities as his *contessa*, and she had confined her life to being the perfect chatelaine, the mother of his heir. His father had taken his son's sympathy for his mother as a reluctance to respect the demands of his heritage, and after his mother's premature death from heart disease, when Cesare was only nineteen, the rift between them had widened without her presence as peacemaker.

But when his father had died, some eight years later, he'd been determined not to neglect any aspect of his inheritance, dedicating himself to its preservation. If his father could see him now, half a dozen years on, perhaps his harsh judgement would be set aside.

The words that he had uttered only that evening, in front of the Luciezo painting of his sixteenth-century forebear, floated in his head.

'Pride in his family, his lineage, his honour—all that he owes his house...'

With the echo of those words his thoughts came full circle back to the woman to whom he had spoken them. Did she understand why he had said what he had about his ancestor—about himself? It was essential that she did. Essential that she understood that, for him, one thing could never change.

In his mind's eye two images formed—the other portraits in the triptych, the Count's wife and his mistress. Separate for ever, coming from different worlds that could never meet.

Four centuries and more might distance him from Count Alessandro and the women who made up the triptych, but for himself, too, his countess would need to share his own background. Not because of any heraldic quarterings she possessed, but because only a woman from the same heritage as himself could truly understand the responsibilities of such a heritage. That was what his father had instilled into him. He had even identified for him the very woman who would make him the perfect next Contessa...

His expression changed and he stared out over the roofs of this most ancient city into whose roots his own ancestry reached. The lineage of a patrician of Ancient Rome was still traceable in his bloodline.

The woman who would be his Countess was well known to him—and she was not, nor ever could be, a woman such as the one he had embraced a brief hour ago, fuelling in him a desire for satiation that he must not yield to.

Not unless—until—he could be sure she accepted what could be between them. And what could not.

As, too, must he. That, also, was essential…

CHAPTER THREE

CARLA STARED AT her screen. She still had six hundred more words to write for her article, and she was making heavy weather of it. She knew exactly why.

Cesare di Mondave.

He was in her headspace—had been totally dominating it, consuming every last morsel of it, since she'd made it into her apartment the night before, senses firing, aflame.

All through her sleepless night she'd replayed every moment of the evening over and over again—right up to that final devastating moment.

Cesare kissing her...

No! She must not let herself remember it again! Must not replay it sensuously, seductively, in her head. Must instead force herself to finish her article, send it into the impatiently waiting sub-editor at her office.

But even when she had she was unbearably restless, her heart beating agitatedly.

Will he phone me? Ask me out again? Or—a little chill went through her—*has he decided he does not want me after all?*

Face set, she made herself some coffee. She should not be like this—waiting for a man to phone her! She should be above such vulnerability. She was a strong-minded, independent woman of twenty-seven, with a good career, as many dates as she cared to go on should she want to, and there was no reason—no *good* reason!—for her to be straining to hear the phone ring. To hear the dark, aristocratic tones of Cesare di Mondave's deep voice.

And yet that was just what she was doing.

The expression in her eyes changed. As she sipped her coffee, leaning moodily against the marble work surface in her immaculate kitchen, more thoughts entered her head. If last night's dinner with Cesare was all there was to be between them she should be relieved. A man like that—so overwhelming to her senses—it was not wise to become involved with. She'd known that from the moment he'd first spoken to her, declared his interest.

But where was wisdom, caution, when she needed them? She felt her pulse quicken again as the memory of that kiss replayed itself yet again.

With a groan, she pulled her memory away. She shouldn't be waiting for Cesare di Mondave to phone her! Not just because she should *never* be waiting around for a man to phone her! But because she should, she knew, phone her mother—reply to her latest complaint about her sister-in-law's disapproving attitude towards her.

She gave a sigh. Her mother—never popular with Guido's younger brother Enrico and his wife, Lucia—had become markedly less popular after her husband's death, when it had become known that the childless Guido, rather than leaving his half of the Viscari Hotels Group shares to his nephew, Vito, had instead left them to his widow, Marlene. They had been outraged by the decision, and when Enrico had suddenly died, barely a year later, his premature death had been blamed on the stress of worrying about Marlene's ownership of the shares. Since then, Vito had sought repeatedly to buy them from Marlene, but Carla's mother had continually refused to sell.

To Carla, it was straightforward. Her mother *should* sell her shareholding to Vito—after all, it was Vito who was the true heir to the Viscari dynasty, and he should control the inheritance completely. But Carla knew why her mother was refusing to do so—her ownership of those critical shares gave her mother status and influence within the Viscari family, resented though it was by her sister-in-law.

Carla's mouth tightened in familiar annoyance. It also continued to feed her mother's other obsession. One that she had voiced when Carla was a teenager and had repeated intermittently ever since—despite Carla's strong objection. An objection she still gave—would always give.

'Mum—forget it! Just stop going on about it! It's never going to happen! I get on well enough with Vito, but please, please, just accept there is absolutely no way whatsoever that I would ever want to do what you keep on about!'

No way whatsoever that she would ever consider marrying her step-cousin...

Vito Viscari—incredibly handsome with his Latin film star looks—might well be one of Rome's most eligible bachelors, but to Carla he was simply her step-cousin, and of no romantic interest to her in the slightest. Nor was she to him. Vito was well known for liking leggy blondes—he ran a string of them, and always had one in tow, it seemed to her—and he was welcome to them. He held no appeal for her at all.

A shiver went through her. She remembered the man who *did*...who'd made every cell in her body searingly aware of her physicality. Who'd cast his eye upon her and then scooped her up into his sleek, powerful car effortlessly.

She felt the heat flush in her body, her pulse quicken. Heard her phone ring on her desk.

She dived on it, breathless. *'Pronto?'*

It was Cesare.

'But this is charming! Absolutely lovely!'

Carla's gaze took in the small but beautifully proportioned miniature Palladian-style villa, sheltered by poplars and slender cypresses, in front of which Cesare was now drawing up. It was set in its own grounds in the lush country-side of Lazio, less than an hour's drive beyond Rome, and its formal eighteenth-century gardens ideally suited the house.

She looked around her in delight as she stepped gracefully out of the low-slung car, conscious of the quietness all around her, the birdsong, the mild warmth of the late-afternoon sun slanting across the gardens—and conscious, above all, of the man coming to stand beside her.

'My home out of town…what is the term in English? Ah, yes…my bolthole.' He smiled.

He ushered her inside, and Carla stepped into a marble-floored, rococo-style hallway, its decor in white, pale blue and gold.

Into her head came a description for the house that was not the one Cesare had just given.

Love nest…

A half-caustic, half-amused smile tugged at her mouth. Well, why *not* a love nest? It was a con-veniently short distance from Rome, and so very charming. An ideal place for romantic dalliance.

Because that was what she was embarking on. She knew it—accepted it. Had accepted it the moment she'd heard Cesare's deep tones on the phone earlier that afternoon, informing her that he would be with her shortly. Taking for granted what her answer would be.

Was she being reckless, to come here with him like this? Of course she was! She knew it, but didn't care. All her life she'd been careful—never one to rush into passionate affairs, never making herself the centre of any gossip. Yet now, a little less than twenty-four hours since she had stood in front of that Luciezo portrait of Count Alessandro, she was going to do just that.

And she would revel in it! For once in her life she would follow the hectic beating of her heart, the hot pulse of her blood, and respond to a man who, like no other she had ever met, could call such a response from her merely by a flickering glance from his dark, hooded eyes. However brief their liaison was to prove—and she knew perfectly well that it could never lead to anything—she would enjoy it to the full until the passion between them burnt itself out, until her desire was quenched.

A man in late middle age was emerging, greeting the Count with respectful familiarity.

'Ah, Lorenzo,' Cesare answered, in a reciprocal tone that told Carla he showed full appreciation of his staff. 'Will you show Signorina Charteris where she may refresh herself?'

Carla was escorted upstairs, shown into a pretty, feminine bedroom, with an en-suite bathroom that had once, she presumed, been a dressing room. As she looked at herself in the glass, checking the careful perfection of her hair and make-up, retouching the rich colour of her lips, for just a second she felt a qualm go through her.

Should I really go ahead with this? Plunge headlong into an affair with a man like this? An affair that can come to nothing?

But that, surely, was why she was doing it! *Because* it could come to nothing! There could be no future with a man for whom marriage to her could never be an option, and therefore love could never be a possibility—never a danger. She would *not* follow in her mother's footsteps, imagining love could come from an affair.

And that is all it will be—an affair. Nothing

more than indulging in the overpowering effect he has on me, such as I have never, never known before.

She could see the pulse beating at her throat, the heightened colour in her cheeks, the quickening shallowness of her breathing. All telling her one thing and one thing only. That it was far too late for any qualms now.

With a quick spritz of scent from her handbag, she headed back downstairs. A pair of double doors stood open now, leading through to a beautifully appointed drawing room with French windows. Beyond, she could see Cesare.

Waiting for her.

At her approach, he smiled, his eyes washing over her with satisfaction.

Yes—he had been right to make the decision he had. This would go well, this affair with this enticing, alluring woman. He had no doubts about it. Everything about her confirmed it. Oh, not just her sensual allure and her responsiveness to him—powerful as it was—but any lingering reservations he might have had about her suitability for such a liaison were evaporating with every moment.

All his conversations with her so far had been reassuring on that score. Though she was Guido Viscari's stepdaughter, she made no special claims on the relationship, which indicated that she would make no claims on the relationship that he and she would share.

Her cool, English air of reserve met with his approval—like him, she would seek to avoid gossip and speculation and would draw no undue attention to her role in his life while their affair lasted—or afterwards. She had a career of her own to occupy her—one that was compatible with some of his own interests—and intelligent conversation with her was showing him that she was a woman whose company he could enjoy both out of bed and in.

She will enjoy what we have together and will have no impossible expectations. And when the affair has run its course we shall part gracefully and in a civilised manner. There will be no trouble in parting from her.

Parting with her...

But all that was for later—much later. For now, the entirely enticing prospect of their first night together beckoned.

His smile deepened. 'Come,' he said, as she walked towards him.

A little way along the terrace an ironwork table was set with two chairs, and there was a stand on which an opened bottle of champagne nestled in its bed of ice. But Carla's eyes were not for that—nor for Cesare. They were on the vista beyond the terrace.

Once more a pleased exclamation was on her lips, a smile of delight lighting her features.

'Oh, how absolutely perfect!'

Beyond the terrace, set at the rear of the villa, a large walled garden enclosed not just a pretty pair of parterres, one either side, but in the central space a swimming pool—designed, she could see at once, as if it were a Roman bath, lined with mosaic tiles and glittering in the sun. Ornamental bay trees marched either side of the paving around the pool, and there was a sunlit bench at the far end, espaliered fruit trees adorning the mossed walls.

Cesare came to stand beside her as she gazed, enraptured.

'We shall try out the pool later,' he said. 'But for now...'

He turned to pour each of them a glass of softly foaming champagne. As she took hers Carla felt the faint brush of his fingers, and the glass trembled in her hand. She gazed up at him, feeling suddenly breathless.

His dark gaze poured down into hers as he lifted his glass. 'To our time together,' he murmured.

She lifted her glass, touching it to his. Then drank deeply from it.

As she would drink deeply from her time with this most compelling of men...

CHAPTER FOUR

THE FIRE WAS burning low in the grate. The long, heavy silk drapes were drawn across the tall windows, cocooning them in the drawing room. Cesare's long legs extended with careless proprietorship towards the hearth from where he sat on the elegant sofa.

The evening had been long and leisurely. Champagne on the terrace, watching the sunset, followed by an exquisitely prepared dinner, discreetly served by Lorenzo in the rococo-style dining room.

Conversation had been easy—wide-ranging and eclectic—and Carla had found it both mentally stimulating and enjoyable, as it had been in the restaurant the night before. As it continued to be now, as she sat, legs slanting towards him, on a silk-covered *fauteuil,* sipping at a liqueur. Coffee was set on the ormolu table at her side…

candles glowed on the mantel above the fire. An intimate, low-lit ambience enclosed them.

Their conversation wove on, both in English and Italian, melding Carla's expertise on High Renaissance art with Cesare's greater knowledge of the politics and economics of the time. And then at some point—she could not quite tell when—the conversation seemed to drain away, and she could not think of one more question to ask him.

Her liqueur was consumed, she realised, and she reached to place the empty glass on the low table at her side. As she released it Cesare stretched out his own hand. Let his fingers slide around her wrist.

It was the first physical contact between them that evening, and it electrified her.

Her eyes went to his, widening at the ripple of sensation that his long, cool fingers circling her wrist engendered. His eyes were on her, heavy and lidded.

Wordlessly, he drew her to her feet. Wordlessly, she let him. Still holding her wrist loosely, he lifted his other hand to her face. Those long, graceful fingers traced the outline of her cheek, her jaw. Faintness drummed in her veins and she felt her body sway, as if no longer able to keep itself upright.

Cesare smiled—a slow, sensual smile. As he had done in the car the night before, just before he'd kissed her. Kissed her as he did now—slowly, leisurely, with infinite sensuality, his mouth like velvet on hers…

'How very, very beautiful you are…' The words were a murmur, a caress. His gaze met hers. His mouth drew free. Her lips were still parted, her eyes still wide and clinging.

'Shall we?' he asked.

She did not answer. Did not need to.

She let him take her upstairs, into the bedroom she'd been shown to earlier, the house hushed around them. Then he was slipping the embroidered evening jacket from her, letting it fall to a chair, sliding down the zip of her dress, easing it from her shoulders. His mouth grazed the bare skin between the cusp of her arm and her neck, and she felt her head move to take in the luxury of his kiss. Slowly she stepped away from him a moment, to step out of her dress, drape it carefully on the chair.

As she turned back she saw that he had carelessly shrugged his own jacket free, and was loosening his tie, slipping the buttons of his shirt. Her eyes went to the smooth, hard wall of his chest. With an instinct older than time she stepped towards him, clad only in bra and panties, and the girdle of her stockings. She saw his eyes flare with male reaction. Felt her own fingertips reach to graze with infinite delicacy across the revealed skin of his torso. Saw his shoulders tense, his pupils become pinpoints.

Wickedly, oh-so-wickedly, she let the palms of her hands slide beneath his shirt, around the warm, strong column of his back, craning her head back to smile into his face with invitation and desire.

For one long, impossible moment he held fast, and still she smiled up at him.

Then, as if a limit had been reached, he gave a low growl in his throat and crushed her to him. His mouth came down on hers and now there was no slow, velvet arousing caress. Now there was only male hunger. Raw, insistent.

Fire flamed in her and her hands flattened on his spine, holding him against her as his mouth devoured hers. Arousal seared in her, her pulse soaring, skin heating. She felt her nipples crest, her breasts engorge—felt, with a fierce flare of arousal, his own arousal against her hips. Sensual excitement filled her...a mad headiness possessed her.

Desire, hot and tumid, took her over—took him over. Possessed them both.

He crushed her down upon the bed, upon the heavy satin covers, and the world was lost to her.

And more than just the world.

Carla twirled around her apartment, her body as light as air, her feet almost off the ground. *Cesare!* Oh, the very name, the very thought of him, filled her being, her mind, every synapse of her utterly possessed existence! How she thrilled to say his name, to see his face, his body—that powerful, sensual, perfect body!—in her mind's eye all the time...

She did not need to be with him to see him. He was there in her head, a constant presence, and every beat of her pulse was telling her what he had done to her.

Their first night together had set her aflame—caught her in a maelstrom of sensation and ecstasy that she had never known possible, that had set her alight with a flame that could not be quenched.

They had stayed at the villa for two days, and Carla had simply blotted out the rest of the world. She'd phoned in to the office the next day, on some pretext or other, to say that she was out of communication, and then she'd turned off her phone and given her entire and absolute focus to the man she was with. To Cesare—who had possessed her utterly, body and mind.

Cocooned at the villa, the only person they'd seen had been Lorenzo, for they had not ventured beyond the formal rooms that she and Cesare had occupied or the gardens beyond the terrace—and the joys of the sparkling Roman-style swimming pool. Where swimsuits had not been necessary…

And making love in the water, beneath the stars

at night, had been a revelation of sensual pleasure such as she had never, never anticipated. She had cried out in ecstasy as he'd held her, cradled her to him, and her head had fallen back, her hair streaming out into the water, her face lifted to the heavens, eyes wide with their reflected glory, as her body had shuddered, and shuddered again, in Cesare's strong possession.

Then, finally, as she'd let her head rest against his shoulder, let the water lap gently around them, he'd waded from the pool, wrapped her in the softest towels and carried her indoors and up to the bedroom—to make love to her all over again...

And again and yet again. Waking and sleeping, sleeping and waking, until the morning sun had streamed through the curtains and he'd been smoothing her tousled hair, smiling down at her.

'Breakfast,' he'd said. 'And then, alas, Rome. I have a lunch meeting I can't get out of.'

Carla had gazed up at him. 'And I must phone my editor.'

She'd smiled, lifting her hand lazily to graze the growth along Cesare's chin. If he grew a beard he'd look even more like his ancestor, she'd found herself thinking, amused.

But amusement had not been uppermost in her thoughts. There had been a stab of fear in the back of her mind—one that had returned as they drove back into Rome later in the morning.

Will he want to see me again—or is this all I shall have of him?

The stab had come again, almost drawing blood…

She'd hidden it, though—had known she must. Known with every instinct of her femininity that making any reference to that at all, asking any such question, would be the very last thing that would help to persuade him that he *did* want to see her again—*did* want more, much more, of what had been between them these last two incredible days.

And so it had proved. As he'd dropped her off at her apartment, he had casually wrapped his hand around her nape, drawn her to his mouth for a farewell kiss. But only farewell for the moment.

'I can't do tonight,' he'd said with a smile, his eyes washing over hers with warm intimacy, 'but the following night is clear. Tell me…how are you with opera?'

Carla had smiled in return, not letting the relief show in her face. 'Very predictable, I'm afraid. Verdi and Puccini, fine, Wagner and modern, not fine—'

He'd laughed and let her go. 'How about Donizetti?'

'*Bel canto* I can cope with,' she'd said in answer, and laughed too.

'Good. Can you meet me before the performance? I'll text you where. We can have a drink beforehand, eat afterwards. How would that suit you?'

Anything—anything would suit me! Anything at all!

The words had soared in Carla's head, but she had not spoken them. Again, instinct had told her otherwise. Instead, she had simply smiled.

'Lovely!' she'd said. And then she'd reached for the door catch, letting herself out of the car as it hummed by the kerb. She'd lifted her hand, given a little wave of farewell. 'See you then,' she'd said airily.

Without looking back again she'd opened the doors to the inner courtyard and stepped inside. Then, and only then, had she clutched at her key and given a crow of joy, of pleasure and relief.

Yes! Yes, he wanted to see more of her, wanted more time with her. Wanted her again... As she—oh, as she wanted him...

Cesare! Oh, Cesare—

His name soared in her head again—filling her mind, her being.

Him and only him...

'How's the article coming along?'

Cesare half twisted his head to call back into the shaded bedroom from where he sat, long legs stretched out in tan chinos, lounging out on the sunlit balcony, his city shirt swapped for a knitted polo, feet in casual, handmade loafers.

Beyond, the darkly glinting waters of Lake Garda hid their glacial depths, reflecting the encircling mountains. He flicked open the tab on the beer he'd just taken out of the minibar in the hotel room. As he sipped its cool flavour his sense of ease deepened. The leisurely weekend ahead beckoned him, and the prospect not just of taking his ease, but of spending it with Carla, bestowed a sense of well-being on him.

The time he spent with Carla always did that to him.

I made a good choice in her. She's worked out well—very, very well.

His eyelids drooped a moment as reminiscence played pleasurably in his head and anticipation of the night to come tonight did likewise. Carla might present a cool, composed front to the world, but when they were alone, when the lights went out... Oh, that was a different matter!

He felt his body quicken in memory. Like a struck match, when he reached for her she went up like a sheet of flame. Passion flared like phosphorous, incandescent and searing. Desire, unleashed, scorched between their bodies...

But it was not that alone—outstanding though it was—that had kept their affair going for so long. It had been six months now, and he showed no sign of tiring of her. But why *should* he tire of her, when passion still ran so strongly? And even when it was exhausted she was so very suitable for him—the ideal woman to have an affair with. She made no attempt to cling to him. Indeed, sometimes he found himself irked by her occasional unavailability, when she cited pressure of deadlines. But he respected her for it all the same. Made no demands on her when she was working.

His eyes shadowed for a moment. His father had shown no such respect for his mother—his mother's role had been to be a docile *contessa*, arranging her life only around the requirements of her difficult husband. Even the weakness of her heart condition had not made his father tolerant of what he perceived as any dereliction in her primary duty to be the chatelaine of his estates.

It was not an attitude he would take when he himself married. Of course his *contessa* would need to be completely willing to play her role as his wife, just as he himself would shoulder the myriad responsibilities of his position, but that did not mean she could have no life of her own as well. In fact…

He snapped his mind away. It was inappropriate to dwell on the qualities his wife would have when he was here with a woman who could never have that title.

And who would not want to.

Nothing about Carla Charteris gave him any cause for disquiet in that respect. And for that he was entirely appreciative. So if, right now, he was having to wait for her to finish her article, then wait he would—as patiently as his temperament permitted.

Some ten minutes later, as he was nearing the end of his can of beer, it was rewarded.

'Finished!' came Carla's voice from inside, with a sense of relief. 'All submitted.'

She lifted the laptop off her knees, closing it down, glancing out towards the darkening balcony. She'd been slightly apprehensive in booking this hotel, in case it did not meet Cesare's exacting standards, but its five-star rating was well deserved. Situated at the lake's edge, its luxury was discreet rather than ostentatious, and a weekend here—following on from her trip to Venice to cover the opening of a new gallery, which had conveniently coincided with Cesare's series of business appointments in Milan—should be extremely pleasant.

Pleasant? The mild word mocked her. The time she spent with Cesare was so much more than 'pleasant'! It was—

Incredible—unbelievable—wonderful—unforgettable!

Her expression softened. Had it really been six months since that first night at his elegant little villa outside Rome? Since then they'd stayed there frequently, recapturing each and every time the scorching intimacy that had swept her away then as never before. Could she have experienced such passion with a man who was *not* Cesare? Impossible—just impossible! He dominated her consciousness each and every day, whether she was with him or not.

Yet she tried hard not to show it—instinctively knowing that any sign from her of being possessive would be fatal. It was that instinctive awareness that told her to be sure never to make any assumptions about him, never to ask him when they would next see each other. Never to rearrange her life for him.

I want to reassure him that he is safe with me. That I do not depend on him. That I have my own life, separate from my time with him.

It was an odd thought, and the reasons she was thinking it were skittering in the back of her mind, trying to land. But she would not let them. Instead, she would enjoy to the max the times they *did* have together—such as this weekend.

She padded on bare feet to the minibar, drawing out a miniature bottle of wine and a glass, then headed out to the balcony, sliding her hands over Cesare's broad shoulders, squeezing lightly.

He turned his head, brushing the tops of her fingers with his mouth. The sensation sent familiar little tremors through her, but she only took a seat beside him on the other sundowner chair, gathering the loose cotton folds of the long printed sundress she'd changed into from her formal Venice outfit, and poured her wine.

'Salute!' he said lazily, and clinked his beer can against her glass.

She returned the toast and took a mouthful of chilled wine, turning to look out over the view. It really was spectacular, and she drank it in as Cesare was doing.

'It's good to see mountains again—though these are a bit too serrated for my tastes,' he heard himself observing, letting his fingers intertwine with hers.

As he spoke, he found himself wondering why he'd made such a remark to Carla. As a rule, he never talked about his own home—even if it was only to contrast the high peaks of the jagged Dolomites with the lower, more rounded Apennines that were the ever-scenic background to the Castello di Mantegna. The *castello* wasn't a place she would ever see, so there was no point mentioning it.

At the thought, a slight frown flickered across his eyes. He crumpled his beer can, tightening his fingers on Carla's.

'Shall we head down to the restaurant?' he said.

He got to his feet, drawing her with him. His eyes went to her. She looked good—but then she always looked good. Always immaculately groomed, with her fantastic figure on show. Wearing what she did now—that loose dress— she looked different somehow. Still a knockout— always that—but more...*medieval*. Her hair was loose too, waving lushly down her back.

A ripple of desire went through him, but he put it aside. That was for later.

They headed downstairs, Cesare carrying her unfinished glass of white wine for her, and in the dining room, which still caught the roseate glow of the lowering sun, they took a table overlooking the lake.

Cesare's sense of well-being deepened. This was good. It really *was* good. Being here, well away from Rome, from home, from responsibilities and social obligations, just having time to himself with the woman he wanted to be with.

How long will I keep this going? This affair... this liaison?

The question wound through his head as they got on with choosing from the menu. The answer came of its own accord.

While it stays good.

* * *

It had certainly stayed good for the rest of their long weekend together.

A sating, fulfilling night together, a slow, leisurely breakfast the next morning, before hiring a car to explore the lake's circuit, and the following day taking a private launch out onto the water itself, lunching on one of the little islands in the lake.

The weekend passed too soon. And it was with regret that he announced at breakfast on Monday morning that he must leave for Milan again.

Carla nodded. 'And I've promised my mother I'll spend some time with her. I've somewhat neglected her these past months.'

Cesare reached for his coffee. As ever, Carla had made no demur at their parting, and he was glad of it. After Milan he must go home—put in some time there, attending to his affairs. His agenda was crowded—the never-ending maintenance work on the *castello* itself, a controversial wind turbine proposal to evaluate, a reforestation project to check up on, a request for the loan of artworks to yet another exhibition to decide on.

Maybe he should discuss that last item with Carla—

He pulled his mind back abruptly. No, that would be a bad move. That might set seeds growing that he did not want to see taking any kind of root. Impossible that they should do so.

Quite impossible.

They drove down towards Milan. Cesare would divert via the airport to let Carla catch her flight back to Rome.

As they drew near, he remarked, 'What would you say to a visit to London?' he asked. 'I'll need to go next month.'

Carla considered. 'I'll have to check my diary,' she said. 'I'm not sure what I've got coming up.'

Cesare nodded. 'Let me know,' he replied easily.

'Will do,' she agreed.

She kept her voice neutral, though inside she felt the familiar flutter of emotion that came whenever Cesare indicated that she was included in his future plans.

Short-term future plans, at any rate.

No, she mustn't think like that. What they had

was good. Very good. Incredibly good. Fantastically good. But—

I don't know what the future will bring. I just don't know. I don't dare know.

She felt a hollowing inside her as the thoughts rushed into her head. Disquieting suddenly, as they echoed again. *Why* should she not dare know…?

An unfamiliar emotion swirled within her, disturbing her by its very presence. And as her eyes went to him now, that hollowing inside her was still there—that disturbing, unidentified emotion that seemed to deepen, to make her gaze cling to his profile as he drove along the *autostrada*, his dark eyes focussed on the road.

As if aware she was looking at him, he glanced sideways a moment. Instantly she schooled her expression. Not noticing the sudden flicker in his eyes before he spoke.

'Do you *have* to be in Rome today?' he said. 'Why not stay in Milan with me? I'll be busy all day, but surely the charms of the *quadrilatera* would while away the hours away for you!' He spoke lightly, knowing that although Carla was always superbly attired, she was no fashionista obsessed with Milan's famous *haute couture* quarter. 'And, of course,' he added, 'there's always the Da Vinci *Last Supper* to look in on!'

That might tempt her more...

He caught himself—was that what he was seeking to do? Tempt her to stay with him now instead of heading back to Rome?

Well, why not? Why shouldn't I suggest she stay with me tonight and head down to Rome tomorrow? It's a perfectly reasonable suggestion.

But that wasn't the reason for his question to himself—he knew that perfectly well. The reason for the question was why he should object in any way to Carla getting back to her own life. Because he shouldn't object—of course he shouldn't. She was her own woman, with her own life, not in the slightest bit assuming that her life was melded to his—and that was very necessary. Essential, in fact, for their liaison to continue.

So why should I need to remind myself of that?

That question was displaced only when he heard Carla's answer. Her tone was a little more clipped than usual, the quick shake of her head infinitesimal.

'I can't, I'm afraid. I've promised my mother, and I don't want to let her down.'

Was there regret in her voice? Hesitation? As if she were reluctant to turn down his invitation to stay with him longer, issued on an impulse he did not wish to scrutinise beyond wanting their mutual enjoyment. If there was, Cesare couldn't hear it. Could only hear her turning his suggestion down.

Could only feel the nip of…of *what*, precisely? Merely annoyance that he was going to have to do without her until they next met up again in Rome? It couldn't be more than that—he would not permit it to be more.

Making himself give a slight shrug of polite regret, he nodded. 'Ah, in that case, then, no,' he murmured courteously.

The turning for the airport was coming up, and he steered off the *autostrada*. Yet after he'd dropped her off he was again conscious of a sense of displeasure. Even regret for himself, that Carla had not stayed with him when he'd wanted her to, despite her perfectly valid reason for not doing so. He would not wish her to neglect her mother for his sake.

Memory flickered in his mind, and he recalled his own mother. How she had always moulded herself around her husband's wishes, whatever they had been, always at his side, always compliant.

It was something he recalled again as, returning home after Milan, he busied himself with the myriad items waiting for him at the *castello*.

Passing the doors of the trophy room—one of a series of staterooms, including the *galleria* containing priceless artworks such as the Luciezo-Caradino triptych—he paused to glance inside. It was his least favourite room, despite its imposing grandeur, for the walls were thick with the antlers and heads of creatures slaughtered by his forebears and added to copiously by his father.

His own open distaste for his father's predilection for slaughtering wildlife had been frequently voiced to his mother, and he'd known she'd shared his disapproval, yet never had she criticised his father. She had acquiesced in that, as she had in everything to do with him, subjugating her views to his on all matters.

Her perpetually acquiescent attitude had both dismayed Cesare and exasperated him.

Cesare's mouth tightened as he walked on into the more recent eighteenth-century part of the *castello*, where the family accommodation was. Every window of the magnificent enfilade of rooms looked out upon terraced gardens and dramatic views over the plunging river valley beyond, framed by the soaring upward slope on the far side that drew the eye to the stony peak of the mountainous summit.

Instinctively, his footsteps took him to the French windows of the drawing room, and he stepped out into the fresh air, drinking in the vista all around him. For a few pleasurable minutes he stood on the terrace in the breeze-filled sunshine, feeling the customary deep and abiding sense of possession of this landscape—this was his home, his domain, his patrimony. And, whatever the dissensions between himself and his father, he had done his best—would always do his best—to prove himself worthy of his inheritance, to shoulder his responsibilities and carry out all the duties of his title and estates.

Including the most critical of all—to establish his new *contessa,* so as to continue the bloodline that stretched far back into the past, to safeguard it for the future. When the time came to take that step—as come it must, one day—his choice of wife would be a wise one—that was essential.

Taking one last deep breath of the crisp, clean air, he went back indoors, made his way to his study at the furthest end of the enfilade. Although the windows gave out onto the same spectacular view he'd enjoyed from the terrace, he schooled himself to turn his attention to the stacks of paperwork neatly piled by his secretary on his desk.

Time to get down to work.

A swift perusal of the files and business correspondence enabled him to select his priorities for the morning, and he was just about to open his emails when his eye caught a glimpse of the handwriting on an envelope in the in-tray containing his personal correspondence. For the most part this consisted of social invitations he would sort through later. But the sight of the handwriting arrested him.

He pulled the envelope out of the pile. Stared down at it a moment. It bore an airmail sticker and a US stamp—and Cesare knew exactly who it was from.

It was from the woman he was destined to marry.

CHAPTER FIVE

'DARLING, HOW LOVELY to see you—it's been such a long time!'

Carla's mother's embrace was reproachful, and Carla felt herself wincing guiltily. It *had* been a long time since she'd spent any amount of time with her mother. Their last meeting had been several weeks ago, and only for lunch while out shopping.

'Well, I'm here now!' she answered lightly, exchanging a careful cheek-to-cheek kiss with her mother. 'And I'm in no rush to leave!'

She would stay at Guido's villa for a few days—it would be at least a week before Cesare was back in Rome and she would see him again.

But you could still be in Milan with him tonight if you'd said yes to him!

The reminder was like a little stab. On the short flight down to Rome she'd replayed that brief exchange a dozen times—and a dozen times wished she'd not given him that short, cool answer. Yet at the time it had seemed essential to say what she had.

I was trying to negate that sudden fear I'd had—fear about why I didn't dare think what my future would be with Cesare. Because I shouldn't feel that—I've always known that there is no future with him. Known that I mustn't care that there is no future.

Known, too, right from the start, that if she wanted any time at all with Cesare she must try not to cling to him, try not to want him too much. He had to know she would never have any expectations of him, never make any assumptions.

Never want a future with him longer than he was prepared to give her.

Or she would have nothing of him at all.

Nothing.

The hollow feeling came again, like a crevasse opening inside her. A crevasse into which that same emotion flared again—more than disquieting, deeper than disturbing.

To have nothing of Cesare—how could I endure that?

No—she tore her mind away. She must not think like this! She was regretting not staying with him in Milan, that was all! Regretting insisting on arriving today at her mother's, even though she could, she knew, have postponed her arrival by a day. It would not have made any great difference to her mother, and she'd have stayed on a day longer to compensate.

I turned down Cesare when I didn't need to.

But she knew why she had done it.

It was to show myself that I don't want to cling to him...don't need to cling to him. To show myself how we are simply having a relationship between adults that we both enjoy, that suits us both. And that is all.

'So...' her mother's voice interrupted her insistent thoughts and she was glad of it '...how was Venice? Tell me about this new gallery that's been opened. Where did you stay? At the Danieli or the Gritti?' she enquired, naming two of the city's top hotels.

As she answered, telling her mother about her

trip there and the article she'd written, Carla welcomed the diversion—welcomed, too, over dinner, letting her mother run on about her social comings and goings, knowing how much Marlene enjoyed her position in Roman society.

Only when all these had been comprehensively covered did Carla ask, casually, after any news of the Viscaris. Vito, she knew, had been on an extensive inspection tour of his European hotels, and was due back in Rome imminently.

'I do hope, Mum,' she ended, casting a significant look at her mother, 'that when he's back here you'll finally agree to sell him Guido's shares…'

The sooner that was done, the better. It had caused a significant rift in relations with her stepfather's brother's side of the family that had rumbled on ever since her stepfather had died.

But immediately her mother bridled. 'Darling, Guido entrusted those shares to *me*! And he had his reasons.'

Carla gave an exasperated sigh. 'Mum, please don't be stubborn! It makes far more sense for Vito to own the entire shareholding—'

The next moment she wished she'd never mentioned the wretched subject.

Her mother's eyes flared. 'Yes, and he could—very easily! Carla, darling, *why* don't you listen to me on this? It would make perfect sense—would be what I've always dreamt of! It would unite both sides of the family! *And* unite the shareholdings as well!'

Carla threw up her hands. Damn, she'd walked into this one!

'Mum,' she said warningly, 'don't go there! I know you've had a thing about it for ever, but please just accept that Vito and I are simply not interested in each other! Not in the slightest! And whether or not Guido left you his shares doesn't change a thing!'

She attempted to put a humorous note into her voice, to defuse the situation.

'Vito wouldn't look twice at me—I'm not blonde, which is the only type of female he ever falls for, and his flashy film star looks just don't do it for me either. I far prefer—'

She stopped short. But it was too late. Her mother pounced.

'Yes, that's *exactly* what I'm concerned about! Darling, are you *mad*?' She leant forward, her expression agitated. 'Cesare di Mondave of all men! I've been hoping and hoping it would just be a brief fling...or whatever you want to call it! But it's been months now and you are still with him! Have you *no* sense?'

Carla shut her eyes, then flashed them open again. Realising with a wash of angry dismay that giving her mother an opportunity to voice her obsession about her marrying Vito had been the least of it!

During the last six months she'd never mentioned Cesare to her mother—had deliberately kept their relationship out of any conversation. The fact that her mother doubtless knew—for Rome was a hotbed of gossip—was no reason to be open with her mother about it. And not just because it didn't play to Marlene's fantasy about finally getting her together with Vito. But because she knew her affair with Cesare would get exactly the reaction she was getting now.

Emotion stormed up inside her. Anger at her

mother, and at herself for walking into this. The last thing she wanted was an inquisition.

'I'm twenty-seven years old—I can handle an affair,' she said tightly.

Her mother's eyes were piercing. '*Can* you?' she said. Her expression changed. 'Darling, it's you I'm thinking of! Affairs can go badly wrong.' She paused again. 'I should know. For me there was no happy ending. And that's what I fear for *you*! There can be no happy ending for you as Cesare di Mondave's mistress—'

Rejection was instant in Carla. '*Mistress?* Of course I'm not his *mistress*!'

Yet even as she rejected the term across her mind seared the memory of that triptych, and the sixteenth-century's Conte's mistress.

I am not that woman—I am nothing whatso-ever like that wretched woman! I am not Cesare's mistress, I am his lover, and he is my lover, and we are together by choice, of our own free will, and I'm perfectly happy with that. Perfectly!

She could see her mother backing off, taking another breath. 'Well, whatever you call yourself it doesn't matter. All that matters to me is that you don't get hurt!'

She shook her head one more time.

'I know I can't stop you, but...' she looked worriedly across at Carla, holding her gaze '...promise me that, whatever happens, when it comes to Cesare di Mondave you won't go and do something unforgivably stupid.' She took a breath. 'Promise me that you won't go and fall in love with him!'

There was silence. Absolute silence. And then Marlene's voice again, sounding hollow now.

'Please promise me that, Carla—*please.*'

But Carla could not answer. Could not answer at all...

Emotion was pouring over her like an avalanche. Wiping the breath from her lungs. Suffocating her with a blinding white truth...

Cesare was out on the terrace, hands curled around the cold stone of the balustrade. Above the gardens and the valley the moon was rising, casting its silver glow over the world. His expression was studied.

Francesca.

Francesca delle Ristori—Donna Francesca— daughter of a *marchese*, granddaughter of a duke on her mother's side, daughter of one of his father's best friends, and ideally suited to be the next Contessa di Mantegna.

Ideally suited to be his wife.

He'd known her all his life. Known her and liked her. And what was not to like? She was intelligent—extremely so—sweet-natured, good-tempered, and, as a bonus, beautiful. She had a pale, ash-blonde beauty that would adorn his arm…that some of their children, surely, would inherit.

Into his head, memory pierced. His father talking to him…*at* him…shortly before the seizure that had killed him.

'She'll be the perfect wife for you—if you've any sense at all you'll see that! She's serious, committed and would be an ornament in her role as your mother's successor!'

It was impossible to disagree with his father's judgement. Francesca would, there was no doubt in his mind whatsoever, make a perfect wife, the perfect next Contessa di Mantegna and mother of the future Count.

When the right time came.

If it was to come at all.

His jaw tightened. That, he knew, was the meat of Francesca's letter to him. Was this long-mooted marriage of theirs to take place—or not? A decision was necessary. And very soon.

And that was the problem he had.

It's come too soon.

As the words formed in his head his inner vision blotted out the moonlit valley before him. He was seeing Lake Garda, sunlight bright on its deep, dark waters, the reflection of the jagged mountains in its surface, seeing his arm casually around the woman beside him as they leant against the stone balustrade on the hotel terrace overlooking the vista.

The memory burned tangibly in him—he could almost feel the soft curve of her hip indenting into his, her hand around his waist. More vivid memory came now, of the last time they had made love, her body threshing beneath his, her mouth hungry for his, her passion released, ardent and sensual, so arousing a contrast with her air of English composure when she was not in his embrace.

I don't want to give that up—not yet.

Oh, one day he would marry—of course he would—but his own preference would have been to postpone marriage for some time. For him there was no necessity to do so yet. But his marriage must be a partnership—with his wife an equal partner. Not for him a marriage like his parents'. His wife would not live the life of his mother, shaping herself around his father's wishes, giving up everything else in her life but her role as Contessa. No, Francesca would be very different—and that included her very understandable desire to marry when the time was right for *her*.

And that time seemed to be now.

He could not ask her to delay—not given the information she had shared with him in her letter. Whatever his reluctance to make that decision now, it had to be done.

He stared out over the valley one long, last time. Slowly, very slowly, his thoughts reached their conclusion. Slowly, very slowly, he exhaled, inclined his head.

Decision made.

In the bedroom that had been hers since her teenage days, up until the time she'd moved out to her own apartment, Carla lay in bed, sleepless, staring up at the painted ceiling. Her eyes were huge, distended. Words ran like an endless litany round and round the inside of her skull—like rats in a trap. Desperately seeking escape.

I'm not in love with Cesare! I'm not! It's just passion—desire—that's all! The way it was from the very start! He makes my heart beat faster just looking at him—but that isn't love! I won't let it be love. I won't.

But even as the litany was repeated she could hear another voice speaking.

So why do you fear not knowing how long he'll want you? Why would you fear a future where you have nothing of him any longer? Why have you kept trying to prove to yourself that you have no need to cling to him, no need to want to be with him more than you are? Why did you make yourself turn down his invitation to stay longer with him today in Milan?

She knew the answer to those questions—knew why she did not want to hear them, did not want to answer them. Did not want to face the truth of what had happened. Fear beat up in her, firing through her veins.

It mustn't be love—what she felt for Cesare, what she felt about him. It just mustn't…

I'm not that stupid! Dear God, I'm not that stupid! To have fallen in love with Cesare di Mondave…

But as the dawn came she knew, with a hollowing of her heart, that what her mother had feared—what she herself had guarded against, right from the start—had happened. And in her head, her mother's warning tolled like doom.

'There can be no happy ending for you—'

A fearful coldness filled her.

CHAPTER SIX

CESARE HANDED THE keys of his car to the valet parker and headed into the restaurant. He was running late, and he knew why. Emotions spiked across his mind, troubling and unwelcome. Tonight was not going to be easy—but it had to be faced. He had to say what he had to say, do what he had to do. No escaping it.

And take the consequences.

Emotion struck again—powerful, like a leopard on a leash. His life was privileged—immensely privileged—but the responsibilities that came with it required a price. A price that he did not wish to pay.

He felt the leashed emotion tug again, bringing to his mind's eye the portrait of his ancestor, Count Alessandro, whom Luciezo had captured for posterity.

You had it easier—you kept your privileges and did not have to pay for them at all!

The triptych was testament to that. The Conte di Mantegna—flanked by his wife and his mistress. And he had kept them both—enjoyed them both. Had had to give up neither—give up nothing at all. Paid no price at all for the life he'd led.

Cesare's jaw tightened. Well, that was then, not now, and now, in this current century, no such arrangement was possible. Not with honour. To marry Francesca meant giving up Carla. No other option.

As he strode into the dining room he saw her immediately. Saw how her blue-violet eyes fastened on his, simultaneously felt another, different emotion seize him.

Her crepe dress in a luscious plum colour graced her full figure, her rich, brunette hair was coiled at her nape, and those lustrous eyes, the generous, sensual mouth, would draw male eyes from everywhere. But her attention was only for him. It had always been that way, and he was accustomed to it.

Yet into his head at that thought came another.

I will have to see her lavishing that same un-wavering attention on another man—another man who will have her to himself...

The thought jabbed in his mind like a spike being driven in. As he reached her, sat himself down, he found himself lifting her hand and dropping a light kiss on it.

'*Mi dispiace.* I was delayed.'

Her smile was instant, and he could see relief in it. But as he looked into her face he could see more than relief. He could see a sudden veiling of her expression. As if she were hiding something from him.

A moment later, though, her expression was open again, her usual air of composure back in place. 'Long day?' she asked sympathetically, starting to skim down the menu.

'Long enough,' Cesare replied.

For the first time with Carla he was conscious of a sense of deceit—it was discomfiting.

He turned the subject away. 'How have you been? Did you visit your mother?'

She nodded with an assenting murmur, but said no more. Cesare did not usually ask after her family—and she never asked after his family affairs. It was an invisible line she did not cross.

The sommelier was approaching, and Cesare turned his attention to him. There was a hollow feeling in the pit of his stomach that had nothing to do with hunger.

Or not hunger for food.

I don't want to do this—I don't want to do it but I have no option. It has to be done, and it has to be done now—tonight.

But not right now. Not over dinner. What he had to say required privacy.

And, besides, I want one more night with her—one last night.

He broke off such thoughts as the sommelier returned, filling their glasses. When he had gone Cesare lifted his glass. That hollow feeling came again.

'To you, Carla,' he said.

His eyes were dark, his expression serious. For a long moment he held her gaze. He saw her face whiten suddenly, her eyes distend. Then, like an opaque lens, he saw her expression become veiled.

Slowly, she inclined her head. 'To you, Cesare,' she replied. Her voice was steady, despite the whitening of her face.

She drank, taking a larger mouthful than she had intended. But right now she needed its fortifying strength. The tension from having waited for him so desperately, overwhelmed by the devastating realisation of what she felt for him, had made her feel faint. Emotion was knifing in her. She felt as if she were seeing him for the very first time.

And I am—I'm seeing him with eyes that see what I have refused to admit until now—what I have guarded myself from for six long months, and what has now overcome me. The truth of what I feel for him.

Weakness flooded through her, dissolving her. Shakily, she lowered her glass to the table, hearing in her head the echo of his simple, devastating tribute.

'To you, Carla...'

That was all he'd said—and yet within her now she could feel emotion soaring upwards like an eagle taking flight from a mountaintop. There

had been such intent in his gaze…such as she
had never seen before.

Can it mean—? Oh, can it mean…?

For a second, the briefest second, she felt an
emotion flare within her that she must not feel—
dared not feel. She crushed it down. It was too
dangerous. Too desperate.

Instead, she watched him set down his glass,
saw the candlelight catch the gold of the crested
signet ring on his little finger. He never removed
it—never. It was there when he made love to her,
when they showered, when they swam. It was
as if it was melded into his skin. Given to him
on his father's death, passed down generation
to generation, one day it would be passed to his
son, the next Conte.

She looked away, back at his face, unwilling
to think such thoughts. Wanting only to drink
him in as a thirsty man in a desert would drink
in fresh water, feeling her heart beating heavily
within her breast. The heart that had so recently,
so devastatingly, revealed its truth to her. The
truth that she *must* not show…

'So, how are things in the Viscari family?'

His casual question made Carla start. She dragged back her hectic thoughts. Collected herself. It was unusual that he was even asking, but she made her reply as casual as she could.

'Vito's heading back to Rome. He's been away for weeks, inspecting all the European hotels.' To her ears, her voice seemed staccato, but Cesare seemed to notice nothing about it. She was glad—grateful.

'Do you get on, the two of you?' Cesare's enquiry was still polite as he demolished the piece of bread roll he'd buttered.

He was not particularly interested, but it was a safe topic of conversation. And right now he needed safe topics.

She blinked, taken aback by his enquiry. Focussed on how to answer it. With a fragment of her mind she registered that Cesare, too, seemed on edge.

'Surprisingly well, really,' Carla answered, sounding, with an effort, more composed now. She made herself go on. 'Considering how my mother and his are usually daggers drawn. She and my mother never hit it off...' She gave a sigh.

'That's often the way between sisters-in-law,' Cesare observed drily. Their first course arrived, and he began to eat. 'Vito Viscari has had a lot to knuckle down to, given the successive deaths of both his uncle and his father. It can be tough. I vividly remember—'

He stopped. Talking to Carla about how he'd had to discover—rapidly—just how to fill his father's shoes after his fatal seizure was not wise.

But Carla did not seem to notice his abrupt cessation. She forked her seafood and nodded.

It was getting easier for her to sound normal, to get her hectic heart rate back under control.

'Because of his ridiculously gorgeous film star looks, people tend to think Vito lightweight—but he isn't at all. I have considerable respect for him,' she said.

Cesare's eyes rested on her a moment. 'And he for you, I hope. After all, you had to contend with arriving in a new country, learning the language, adapting to a new way of life.'

'Vito was very kind to me,' she answered, her voice warming. 'Helped me settle in. Improved my Italian, took me about with him to meet his friends. Warned me off several of them!' she finished with a laugh.

The laugh had sounded quite natural to her ears, and she was again grateful.

Cesare smiled. But he knew it was something of a forced smile. There had been a fond note in her voice, and he had not liked to hear that. Nor did he like to examine *why* he had not liked to hear it.

'Would he have warned you off me?' he heard himself asking.

He'd kept his voice light, deliberately so, masking that slight jab that had come when he'd heard her praising her step-cousin so affectionately—yet he was aware that he had asked the question. *Why* he had asked it.

For all his light tone, he saw her face still. The expression in her eyes changed.

'He would not have needed to, Cesare,' she said quietly. 'I've always known the score with you. Credit me with that much, at least.'

His eyes shifted away, his jaw tightening. Then, abruptly, his gaze came back to her. She was looking at him, again with that veiled expression in her eyes. Impulsively he reached for her free hand, raised it once more to his lips. This was the last night of his life that he would spend with her—he would not stint on his appreciation of her. Of what she had been to him.

What she can be no longer.

He felt again that jab of regret that it should be so. More than a jab. Yet again the words sounded in his head.

Not yet.

But there was no point thinking that—none. He must part with her, and that was all that was possible now. That—and this one last, final night with her.

'I credit you with a great deal, Carla.'

There was emotion in his voice. She could hear it. And inside she felt again that sudden flare of emotion that she had felt when he'd raised his glass to her, let his gaze rest on her with such intent.

She returned his gaze now, as he let go of her hand and it fell to the table. Her breath seemed dry in her lungs.

Why had he said that? Why was he acting the

way he was tonight? There was something about the way he was being that she had never seen in him before.

What does it mean?

She swallowed, feeling her cheeks flush suddenly. Dipped her head to resume her meal. Yet through her consciousness her mind was racing. That same swooping sensation was within her. Cesare was different tonight. She could see, could tell—knew with every instinct that something was changing between them. Something profound that would alter everything...

Can it be—can it really be? After all, if I was in denial for so long, if I told myself over and over again I could not possibly feel love for him... could it be that maybe, just maybe, for him it's the same?

The thoughts were barely there, barely allowed, barely shaped into words—for she dared not let them be. Dared not give in to the swooping, soaring inside her as their meal progressed, as emotions swirled and formed and dissolved within her.

How *could* she dare? How could she dare give

in to the one emotion above all that she yearned to give in to?

How could she give in to hope?

Hope that he might just feel for me what I now know I feel for him... That—despite everything— he's fallen in love with me too?

'A miracle—a parking space!'

Carla's exclamation was heartfelt. To find a free parking space on her narrow street was, indeed, a miracle. Yet there it was.

Is it a sign—can it be a sign?

She almost laughed at herself for the notion, yet knew with a fragment of her mind that she was not joking at all.

As Cesare expertly parallel parked in the confined space, she could feel yet again her emotions soaring within her. For hope was a bird that, once released, could not be imprisoned again.

Throughout the evening, Cesare's air of particular attentiveness to her had been palpable, that sense of something different about him unmistakable.

Now, as they climbed out of the car and she

opened the outer door to let them both into the inner courtyard, his closeness to her was even more palpable.

Upstairs in her apartment she went into the kitchen to set the coffee brewing. Usually when he stayed over with her he settled down on the white sofa, his long legs reaching out, and shrugged off his jacket and tie, happy to lounge with her while drinking coffee, and sometimes a liqueur, before arousal took them both and swept them off to bed.

Tonight, however, he followed her into the kitchen.

'Do you really want coffee?'

She turned. He was standing there, and in his eyes was an expression that wiped all thought of coffee from her mind—all thought at all. An expression that was all too familiar to her. Slowly she shook her head. For one long, timeless moment she did not move, and nor did he. Something flowed between them. Something that took her back to that very first night they'd spent together.

The villa outside Rome, Cesare's love nest, had

seen much use in the months since then. But at this moment all she could think of was that very first night.

Warmth beat up in her. Suffusing her skin, flaring out from her core. He stepped towards her, curved his long fingers around the nape of her neck, drawing her towards him. But not into his arms. He held her in front of him while his other hand rested lightly around her waist. His dark, lidded eyes held hers, unfathomable, unreadable.

Turning her bones to water.

She felt emotion rise up in her like a sweeping tide, pouring through her. Her lips parted and there was a low, frail noise in her throat.

'Cesare—' His name was like a whisper in her mouth…an echo deep within her.

The knowledge of what she now knew she felt for him had ripped across her like a revelation and it trembled within her. It was making her tremble again now as the thumb of the hand at her nape reached forward to graze the cusp of her jaw, stroked the hollow below her ear in a soft, sensual caress that sent a thousand feathers fluttering through her veins.

'You are so, so beautiful,' he said.

Slowly, infinitely slowly, as if he were savouring every long moment of its descent, he lowered his mouth to hers. For one long, timeless moment, his kiss was nothing more than a velvet graze along her lips. Then, with a rasp in his throat, he tightened his fingers at her nape, his hand at her waist, and hauled her to him hungrily, ravenously.

As though she were the last meal he would ever eat.

Like a sheet of flame she went up in an inferno of sensation, of passion and desire, white-hot and incandescent. With absolute mastery he possessed her mouth and then, feasting his way down, he swept her up, clamping her against him as he strode from the kitchen, pushing open the door of her bedroom, coming down on the bed beside her.

Clothes were shed, bodies were arching, limbs twining, mouths meeting and melding. Bodies fusing.

Fusing with that same white heat, that same incandescence. She cried out over and over again, her body shaking. The ecstasy he wrought on her was unbearable, meeting for the first time the flood of emotion that poured through her, the knowledge of what it was he meant to her...

The man she loved. Cesare—oh, Cesare—the man she loved.

The knowledge of it, the certainty and the rapture of it, was a possession of her heart and of her soul even as she gave him possession of her body, took possession of his, giving to him all that was within her. It was a glory, a dedication of herself to him without measure, without reserve. An absolute oblation of herself...

And at the end, as wave after wave of shuddering ecstasy and love finally ebbed from her, she held him in her arms, crushing him to her. His dampened skin cooled, his hectic breathing calmed, and she wrapped herself around him, half cradled by him, their limbs tangled and exhausted. She knew, with certainty and utter conviction, that she had never known happiness until this moment. Never known until this moment what love truly felt like.

She held him close against her, smoothed the

strong contours of his powerful back. Wonder filled her—and a gratitude beyond all things. He had cried out as the moment had possessed him, as if it had been the very first time they had made love. The intensity of it had shaken her, overwhelmed her.

It could mean only one thing—surely only one thing? His passion for her had been greater than he'd ever shown, his response more searing than she had ever known it to be, his fulfilment fiercer, more burning than she had ever seen before. And now, as she lay with him, his arms around her were tighter than she had ever known.

As if he would not let her go.

As if he would *never* let her go…

As if she were his and he was hers for ever now…

For ever…

Eyelids fluttering, she felt the great lassitude of her body sweep over her, and sleep took her.

She awoke alone. In the bathroom she could hear the shower running. For a few moments she lay, languorous, her mind in a dream state. Wonder still suffused her—like an underground spring filling the receptive earth. Happiness—rich, and full and glorious—ran in her veins like cream. She had never been happier in her life.

Because of Cesare—oh, Cesare, Cesare, Cesare! The world was new-made, new-found. Illumined by love, by joy, by glory.

The shower was cut off. A moment later Cesare was walking into the bedroom, a towel snaked around his hips. He walked quietly, as if not wanting to disturb her. She went on lying there, immobile, watching him through shuttered eyes only just affording vision.

She watched him dress swiftly, surely, fastening his cuffs, knotting his tie—all the tiny, familiar minutiae of the morning. She felt a vague disappointment, for clearly he had an appointment to get to. But then, *she* had to attend an editorial meeting that morning anyway, and a lunch afterwards, so she did not mind him leaving her like this. There would be tonight—and the night after, and all the nights thereafter. The future was stretching ahead of them. She was sure of it, certain of it.

How could it be otherwise now?

Now that I know I love him.

For now, with love pouring through her, she knew, above all, that she could dare to hope.

Whatever it is he feels for me he does *feel for me! I am more to him than I was! I know it—oh, I know it, I know it!*

Give him time—just give him time. Make no demands, be as cautious and as careful as ever. But with time—oh, with time he will come to feel more for me. Whatever might happen...

There were no certainties about him, but there *were* possibilities. Oh, that much she must have faith in. She must and she could—and she did.

Her mother's warnings seemed a thousand miles away—as did her own warnings, issued to herself all her life, all these months with Cesare.

I can believe in my happy ending—I dare to believe in it! I dare to hope! To have faith in my heart...in his...

Her love could make it happen—she needed only hope and faith. And both were streaming through her as her eyes drank him in, her heart overflowing with wonder and gratitude. With joy.

He crossed to the bed, sat down on it, his hand reaching for her shoulder as if to wake her. She opened her eyes—opened them and smiled, lifting her hand to catch his. For a second he let her, then her lowered her hand to the sheet, taking his own away. His face was expressionless.

Out of nowhere, like a knife sliding into her guts, fear gouged inside her.

'Carla, there is no easy way to say this...'

His voice was deep, with a tension in it that cut like a wire through flesh. His mouth was compressed, and she could only stare at him, motionless and frozen, while inside the fear widened into a chasm, swallowing her.

He took a breath, got to his feet. Stood tall and powerful, looking down at her. Remote and distant.

'This is the last time I can see you,' he said. 'In a few days I shall be announcing my engagement.'

He looked down at her. His eyes had no expression in them at all.

'I didn't want you hearing it from anyone else. Roman gossip is vicious.' He paused again, his mouth tightening yet more. 'I want you to know…'

And now, for the first time, there was something in his eyes—something that only plunged that knife into her yet deeper, with a serrated, twisting blade, eviscerating her.

'I want you to know how good these last six months have been. How…very good.'

He turned away. Reached her bedroom door.

'I'll see myself out.'

There was another pause, a whitening around his mouth.

'Look after yourself, Carla.'

Then he was gone, and she could hear him walking across her living room, reaching her front door. For a second, an infinity of horror, she froze. Then, muscles bunching, she hurled herself from the bed like a tornado, tore after him. Naked—completely naked. As naked as her soul.

Her eyes blazed like furnaces. A single word shot from her.

'Why?'

He turned. There was no expression in his face. It was tight and closed as the great oaken doors of his *castello*. Guarding him against all who might invade. He had not let *her* invade. Would not permit her to do so.

He answered her now, his voice steady, unemotional. As it had to be. As it was essential for it to be. He would tell her what he had had to tell himself. Rigid discipline held him to his course, as if he were urgently steering his car out of an aquaplane that would otherwise send him crashing down into a bottomless crevasse.

This had to be done. It had to be said—*had* to.

'You said yourself, Carla, that you've always known the score with me. As I said, I gave you full credit for that.' He took a breath. 'Full credit for understanding *"why".'* His mouth thinned. 'I have to marry. I've always had to marry. I've always had an…understanding…'

Was there irony in his repetition? He was beyond irony—beyond everything right now except knowing that his only urge was to get away, not to see her standing there, her body naked—the body he had possessed. Still wanted to possess…

'An understanding,' he said, 'for many years. And whilst my…my fiancée…' He said the word as if it were alien to him, in a language he did not comprehend, had never needed to speak till now. 'My fiancée has shared that understanding, she has had her own interests to pursue till now. She's been living in America, but now she needs to decide whether to stay there…or come home. To fulfil the…the understanding…we have always had.'

He took another breath. Every word he was speaking seemed to be impossible to say. It was a clash of worlds and he was crushed between them.

'She's now made her decision, and it is to return to Italy. Therefore…' he swallowed '… I must part with you. I apologise that I could not give you more warning, but…' He took another heavy breath. 'She's flying to Italy tomorrow, to visit her parents, and naturally they will want to hear her decision. And then…' His expression changed again. 'Then they will all be visiting me at the Castello Mantegna, where our engagement will be formally announced.'

She stared at him.

Her eyes were stretched, distended. 'Do you love her?'

It seemed the only question she could ask. The only one in the entire universe.

Her voice was thin, like wire pulled too fine. It grated—grated on him. What place had 'love' in his life? None that he could permit.

A look of impatience, of rejection, passed over his face. 'Love is an irrelevance. Francesca and I are...well-suited.'

For a second—just a second—his eyes searched hers. He took a breath, forcing himself to say what he did not want to say, did not want to face.

'Carla, if you have ever fancied yourself to feel for me anything at all...' His mouth tightened, his hand on the doorjamb clenching. 'You must know I never invited any such feelings from you—never consciously or unconsciously sought them. I never, Carla, gave you any indication whatsoever that there could be anything between us other than what has been. Acquit me of any accusations to the contrary. We had an affair. Nothing more. It could never have been anything more. You knew that as well as I.'

Long lashes dipped over his lidded, expression-less eyes—eyes that slayed her like a basilisk's lethal glance.

'I must go,' he said.

And he went.

Walked through the door. Leaving her. Closing the door behind him.

The noise seemed to echo in the silence. A silence that spread like toxic waste after the deadly poison of his words to her. That lasted until, time-less moments later, a strange, unearthly keening started in her throat…

'Carla! Open the door!'

Her mother's voice came on her voicemail. Continued loudly.

'I am not leaving here until you do. Just open it!'

Carla heard her, heard the sharp, demanding rap come again on her front door. Her mother would not go—she knew she wouldn't. Her mother's will was unbreakable.

She walked to the door, opened it, and her mother surged in.

Then stopped.

'Oh, dear God,' Marlene said, her voice hoarse.

She stared, horrified, at Carla, and Carla knew why. Her hair was unbrushed, she was wearing a tracksuit, not a trace of make-up. Her eyes were red, cheeks blotched. There were runnels running down from her eyelashes to her chin, where tears had been shed and had dried, shed and dried.

For two whole days.

Her mother's hand had gone to her mouth in disbelief, but now she lowered it.

'So, it's true, then?'

Carla looked at her. 'I take it the gossip has started already?'

Marlene drew in a breath sharply. 'Oh, yes,' she said. 'And *several* of my acquaintances have made absolutely sure I knew about it!'

Carla turned away. Tears had started again—but to what purpose? To what purpose was anything at all?

Her mother was speaking, her voice harsh, vicious, but she paid no attention.

She warned me, and I didn't listen. 'No happy ending,' she told me—but I thought I knew better.

She felt her face convulse, her throat constrict as if a snake were strangling her, its coils thrown around her body, tighter and tighter, crushing the life out of her, the breath.

She felt her mother's arms come around her, but what comfort could they bring? What reassurance? What help?

None. None, none, *none*.

Bitterness filled her, and self-hatred.

No happy ending...

She shut her eyes, resting her head against her mother's shoulder as her mother went on speaking, saying things she might say to a child, patting her back, rubbing it as if she could make her better. But there was no 'better', no happiness, no nothing. Only memories stabbing into her, over and over again, each one eviscerating her, taking out a little more of what she was made of.

Dear God, I thought—I really, really thought—that he was being different that night in the restaurant because he was starting to feel something for me! I thought that there might be possibilities of his returning what I'd just discovered I felt. I

*actually started to hope...to believe in a future
for us...to believe in love between us...*

Anguish clutched at her, its icy hand around
her heart. Her stupid, stupid heart.

*Why did I have to go and realise what had hap-
pened to me? Why did I have to discover what
I'd come to feel for him? If I hadn't—if I'd still
thought it was only an affair and nothing more
than that—I wouldn't be here like this now...
destroyed...just destroyed.*

'You told me...you told me—*no happy ending.*'

She must have spoken. Words must have
scraped past her lips. Her voice seemed to come
from very far away, from polar regions where icy
winds blasted her to pieces.

No happy ending.

She felt her shoulders taken, saw her mother
step back from her, still holding her. Carla looked
at her face, and what she saw made her stare.

'But what there *could* be,' Marlene said, biting
out each word, her eyes suddenly as bright and
hard as diamonds, 'is a *better* ending.'

She dropped her hands. The diamond brightness in her eyes was glittering now, her face as hard as crystal.

'There's only one way to do this, my darling girl. Only one! When a man does to you what that…that *swine*…has done to you, there is only *one* thing to do!'

She sat down on the sofa, patted the seat next to her.

'Sit down, Carla, and let me put something to you.'

CHAPTER SEVEN

CESARE'S VOICE WAS warm as he greeted the guests being ushered into the drawing room at the *castello*—the Marchese and the Marchesa and their three adult children—Francesca and her younger brother and sister.

Francesca he'd already met up with, as she'd requested, on her own, when she'd arrived back in Italy. They'd talked, long and in detail, feeling their way forward, reaching a mutual understanding. Now she was here at the *castello* with her family to formalise that understanding.

Their greetings were cordial and affectionate. He'd known her family all his life, just as he'd known Francesca—though he'd seen little of her since she'd gone to the States to do her postgraduate studies four years ago. Only occasional meetings when he'd been out there on business and taken the opportunity to look her up, or when she was visiting Italy from time to time.

There had been no rush—no need to meet up more.

He'd hoped that he could go on like that for a while longer still.

Into his head stabbed an image—he thrust it from him. He'd been thrusting it from him for days now. It was essential to do so. Absolutely essential.

Carla is in the past. I have made my decision. I will not rescind it. I cannot—

Because it would be impossible to do so. Impossible now that Francesca was here, with her family, for the intimate gathering that would result in their formal engagement. The engagement he was entering into entirely of his own volition. His own preference. The engagement that had always been waiting for him. That would now be fulfilled.

Putting Carla behind him for ever.

Greetings over, he signalled that the champagne should be served. His staff were excited, he could see, for this was to be their new chatelaine—the new Contessa. They approved of his choice—and what was there not to approve of? Francesca had visited here often—with her parents, as a child, as a teenager and as an adult.

Now, as she sipped the vintage champagne, Francesca looked tall and serene in a Grecian style off-white gown that matched her ash-blonde hair, her pale, slender beauty—very different from Carla's full-figured, vivid looks.

Carla…whom he would now never see again—except perhaps on rare social occasions if their paths should cross in Rome. But never again would she be what once she had been to him.

I wanted longer with her.

The guillotine sliced down again. Sliced through the thought and the image that formed in his head of Carla at her most alluring. He must not think of her—must *not*. Francesca was saying something to him and he must pay attention to her, ask a question in return. Something about her work that he hoped was not too unintelligent. But her field of research was so rarefied he knew he could only stumble at its edges.

She smiled, giving him an explanation he

could understand. Behind her, her father beamed proudly, and her mother bestowed a doting look upon her.

'A doctor of science!' her father said, with pride openly in his eyes. 'And achieved two years before it was expected!'

'Astrophysics!' breathed her mother.

Cesare shook his head ruefully. 'I'm humbled even by the thought of it!' he exclaimed lightly.

Francesca gave a laugh. 'Oh, Ces—you? Humble? You've never been humble in your life!'

'Before *your* intellect, how can I be otherwise?' he rejoined promptly.

His eyes rested on her. She truly was a remarkable woman—extreme intellect, glowing beauty and an ancestry that wound throughout the annals of Italy's history.

She will make an exceptional contessa*!*

His father had been right—irrefutably right—in his judgement of Francesca delle Ristori. Only one aspect had he neglected—and that was what Francesca had needed to discuss with him so deeply.

Cesare had heard her out, given her all the assurances she required, let her choose entirely by herself whether she was going to do as she had now chosen—be his wife. He had assured her that of course there would be no question—none at all—of her having to focus solely on her role as his *contessa* as his mother had. She would join whatever research facility suited her field here in Italy, for as long as she wanted to, and find fulfilment both as his *contessa* and as a research scientist.

Francesca would *not* be the kind of wife his own mother had had to be—of that he was completely sure. He didn't want that—and nor would Francesca have contemplated marriage to him on any other basis.

He drew her out a little over dinner, and she smiled and mentioned some possibilities of where she might work in Italy.

'I need to see how my doctoral research paper is received,' she said. 'Its reception may determine what offers I'm made, and by whom.'

'I'm sure they will be clamouring for you from all quarters!' he said gallantly.

Francesca laughed, and so did her parents and siblings.

The meal passed in similar convivial fashion. Everyone was pleased. Her parents were highly satisfied—for them, their daughter's marriage to him would ensure she stayed in Italy, and that was their preference. Francesca seemed pleased too, and he was glad of it. Her choice had not been made without inner conflict, but she had made it all the same. And in his favour.

And as for him—well, of *course* he was pleased. How could he not be? How could anyone not wish for Francesca as his bride, his wife, his *contessa*, the mother of his children, the companion of his life, his entire future…

Just as he'd anticipated, all his adult life…

The image he had banished earlier came into his head again, like a spectre haunting him.

Carla…

He sliced it off at source. Asked another question about astrophysics.

The evening ended.

Francesca and her family repaired to the guest quarters.

He would woo her later—do all that was necessary between them to make her comfortable with him in that respect. Their respective pasts were irrelevant. With the decision made between them, all prior involvements would be severed. Terminated.

That guillotine sliced again.

Ruthless. Lethal. Permanent.

Because it had to be.

Carla stood, her back stiff, her face stiff, talking, sipping mineral water, refusing canapés, posing for photos. Her mother was entertaining—*fare uno mostro*—putting on a show, as she so loved to do.

This time it was for the director of a museum to which some of the choicest pieces of Guido's extensive collection were being donated. Her mother was in her element, Carla could see, being very much the gracious hostess, the generous patroness of the arts.

Across the large salon in her stepfather's opulent villa Carla could see her step-cousin, Vito, only that day arrived back in Rome from his tour of the European hotels, with his mother, Lucia. The latter looked icily furious, the former was visibly 'on duty'.

Carla had said very little to him during the evening. She was not in a talkative mood.

The reception went on and on. There were speeches—her mother's, in careful, laboured Italian, and then Vito stepping forward, clearly intent on representing the official side of the Viscari family. And there was posing for more photos, herself included, standing right next to Vito. The only saving grace was that she would not be writing this up—that would be too nepotistic.

Anyway, she hadn't been to work for days now. Citing a bug…a touch of flu.

Whether anyone believed her or not, she didn't care. She doubted the gossips did. They knew *exactly* why she was out of circulation.

Her mouth tightened.

Francesca delle Ristori—that was what Cesare's bride-to-be was called. The gossip columns were already full of open speculation. And after all, why not? What was there *not* to speculate about?

A vicious light glared in Carla's eyes.

She's the granddaughter of a duke, the daughter of a marchese, *a family friend from for ever—she has long fair hair down to her waist and she has a PhD in astrophysics! Dear God, is there anything she hasn't got?*

But there was only one thing she wanted Francesca delle Ristori *not* to be—only one.

Cesare's fiancée.

The knife thrust again into her guts. Eviscerating her. Her hands clenched at her sides.

People were leaving—finally. From her immobile position she saw her mother and Lucia go through a poisonous little ritual of one upmanship about the evening's success, then her mother was graciously inviting her sister-in-law and Vito to stay and take coffee with her, to hear all about Vito's recent travels. Adding, portentously, that they really must settle the business of Guido's shares…

Immediately, Vito tensed, Carla could see, and exchanged looks with his mother. Then promptly offered to escort his mother to her car, while he returned for coffee. The mention of Guido's shares—half the family shareholding—was a bait Vito would not be able to refuse. How could he? His determination to acquire the shares, giving him total control of the hotel chain as the sole Viscari left, was paramount. The shares her mother had adamantly refused to sell.

Now, walking with punishing stiffness, Carla followed her mother into the drawing room, taking up a stance behind her mother's chair. Vito strolled in, having said farewell to his mother—doubtless sympathising with her for the ordeal they'd both endured, with Marlene queening it over them as Guido's widow.

Well, she didn't care. Didn't care about Lucia's irritation, or Vito's frustration over the shares, or her mother's endless manoeuvrings. She cared only about one thing.

It burned inside her like hell's furnace. Her hand tightened, spasmed over the back of her mother's chair. Her mother was talking, but Carla wasn't listening. Vito was answering, but she wasn't listening to him either. The barbed exchange went on, but she paid it no attention.

Not until the moment came. The moment her

mother had planned for, schemed for, hoped for, for so long now. The moment Carla had never in a thousand years thought she would collude with.

As she did now.

She heard her mother talking to Vito, her tone saccharine. 'What could be better than uniting the two Viscari shareholdings by uniting the two halves of our family? You two young people together!'

Silently, she watched Vito's reaction. Saw angry disbelief lash across his face. Didn't care. Didn't care at all. Saw his furious gaze snap to her, demand she answer—demand she shoot down immediately what her mother had just said. Refuse, outright, the preposterous notion Marlene had put forward.

She refused to think of the devastating, demolishing impact on her step-cousin.

The agonising pain of Cesare's brutal rejection had caused a consuming need to hit back at him, to claw around her raw and ravaged heart the tattered, ragged shreds of her own pathetic pride any way she could—no matter who paid the price for it, no matter how vilely it made her behave.

'I think,' she heard herself say, from somewhere very far away, where icy winds scoured all emotion from her, 'that's an excellent idea.'

The next days passed in a choking blur. Carla blanked everything and everyone. Refused to talk, refused to face what she was doing. She was like one possessed by an evil spirit, with the devil driving her.

Vito, getting her away from Marlene, had railed at her disbelievingly. Then he'd done worse than rail. He had realised why she was playing to her mother's obsession. His expression had said it all as the reason for her collusion with her mother dawned on him.

'So that's it—he's finished with you, hasn't he?'

Vito's pity had lacerated her, like thorns scraping her flesh. Then he'd poured acid on the wound.

'To speak frankly, it was always going to end that way. The Conte di Mantegna can trace his bloodline back to the ancient Romans! He's going to marry a woman who can do the same! He might have affairs beforehand, but he'll never marry a woman who—'

'A woman, Vito, who is about to announce her engagement to another man!' The words shot from her as from a gun.

Because that—*that*—was the truth of it! That was the poisonous salvation that her mother had put to her that unbearable morning in her apartment. *That* was how she was going to survive what Cesare had done to her—what she had done to herself. Falling in love with a man who was marrying another woman. A woman so much more *suitable* to be his wife than she was! A woman, so the gossip columns were already saying, who was utterly perfect to be the next Contessa di Mantegna.

As she herself had not been.

Worse than the words in the fawning articles had been the photos of Cesare and Francesca delle Ristori—smiling, elegant, aristocratic, such a perfectly matched couple!

Worse again than that were the photographs of herself and Cesare—taken, so she supposed in her embittered misery, at any time during the last six months at restaurants and art galleries—or of herself alone, the photos that accompanied her articles.

And the prurient, goading words that went with them, contrasting her with Cesare's noble-born fiancée.

One-time constant companion...
Another shapely beauty to adorn the arm of our dashing, illustrious Conte di Mantegna...
Daughter of late hotelier Guido Viscari's English wife, co-owner of the Viscari luxury hotel chain.

Well, it was *that* that was going to save her! Save her from the unbearable humiliation that crushed her, from the mockery of the world—and herself.

You fool—you pathetic fool! To have thought—to have really believed—that that final night with him was the start of something more! That he was feeling for you what you had realised you felt for him! When all along...

Her mind twisted away and the scorpion whips

lashed again. Wielded by the devil that was driving her now, along the desperate path she was taking. But she would take it all the same, and wouldn't care what she was doing to Vito, wouldn't care that he hated her for it, would not *let* herself care.

She would only forge on with it, frantic to cling to the only thing she *could* cling to—getting her own engagement announced to stop the pitying comments, the veiled sneers, the less than veiled gossip, targeting her as the discarded former *inamorata* of the noble Count now set on marrying his noble bride...

Because no one, *no one*, would pity her or sneer at her when she was the wife of one of the most eligible bachelors in Rome! When her husband was the multi-millionaire Vito Viscari with his film star looks, fêted and courted by all, a major European corporate player, and when their marriage had united the ownership of a global hotel chain!

Because if Cesare di Mondave could make a dynastic marriage—well, so could *she*! And her marriage to Vito would show Cesare she cared as little about him as his engagement to the beautiful Francesca delle Ristori showed that *he* cared about the woman he'd spent the last six months with! Show him that their time together had been nothing more than a pleasant interlude for *both* of them, before they'd *both* taken up their destiny—he to marry his aristocratic bride, she to unite the two halves of the Viscari family.

But she *had* to get her engagement to Vito announced formally! She had to make it happen—was desperate for it!

The devil drove her on, his reins steering her remorselessly, unpityingly.

Yet still Vito held out.

Balked at committing to her.

Wanted to reject her—just as Cesare had rejected her!

He had no desire to marry her—just as Cesare had no desire to marry her!

Desperation and despair possessed her, darkening her vision. She *had* to get Vito to publicly commit to her—by *any* means. Any at all—whatever it took.

Carla could see that as plain as day through the

dark flames in her vision. Her mother saw it too. Took steps. Rumours flew—were Guido's shares for sale? If so, to whom?

The financial press ran with the story, just as her mother had intended. Rival hotel chains' names were speculated. Nic Falcone, his long-time competitor, was the front runner, keenest to snap up the oh-so-enticing Viscari shares. Yet still Vito would not agree to announce their engagement—now he was saying there was already a woman in his life, an Englishwoman he'd met on his European tour, whom he'd brought to Rome and who was staying at the Viscari Roma.

So Carla paid a visit there. Found the beautiful, long-legged blonde who was so clearly besotted with Vito. Told her that she was no one special—*like I was no one special to Cesare*—that Vito would have finished with her soon enough anyway—*like Cesare did me*—and with every stinging, bitter, galling truth, a knife went into her own heart, twisting in agony. And when Vito turned up, full of angry denunciation of what she'd said, she defied him to deny it—defied him to say she was *not* his fiancée. He could not—

not if he wanted her mother's shares, if he valued them more than the tearful woman clinging to his chest, sobbing…

The blonde's despairing sobs tore at Carla, tore at her own throat, but she would not recant her words. Found justification for them in her own misery and torment.

It's better she knows now what's important to Vito—and it's not her!

Just as *she* had not been important to Cesare…

The devil's scorpion whip lashed at her again, driving her onwards as she dragged Vito away, forcing him on along the dark path she was treading, her eyes glittering with desperate fervour. Damning herself and everyone around her.

CHAPTER EIGHT

CESARE STOOD IN the massive fortified gateway that led to the walled courtyard of the *castello*, watching the Marchese's car wind its stately way down the hairpin road snaking into the valley below. Then he turned away, walked back into the *castello*.

The visit of Francesca and her parents had been a complete success, and now she was going with her parents to the family seat in the north of Italy before flying back to the USA to settle her affairs there.

There was no immediate rush for them to marry—the date was set for late summer, and Francesca's mother was intent on enjoying every moment of the lavish preparations. Also, Francesca wanted to see if she could secure a post-doctoral position at a physics department in Italy. When she returned from America, visited the *castello* once more, Cesare would start to take her out and about with him on prenuptial social engagements. Start his personal courtship of her, the woman who would be his bride.

As the woman he had set aside could never be.

Could never be in his life again in any way.

As it always did, the guillotine sliced down in his head. That subject was still not safe. With iron self-discipline—a self-discipline that he seemed to need increasingly now, but which, surely to God, would fade as time passed—he put aside the thoughts he must not have, the memories he must not recall.

He strode indoors, but as he did so, he glanced up the massive oak staircase that led to the upper floor of the staterooms. That floor was dominated by the full-length *galleria*, once the exercise space for the ladies of the house in bad weather, which now contained the bulk of the artworks here at the *castello*.

Including the Luciezo-Caradino triptych.

As if impelled, Cesare felt himself heading towards the base of the stairs. Then, abruptly, he pulled away. No, he would *not* go and look at it.

To what purpose? He knew what it looked like. Knew why he wanted to go and look at it.

His expression steeled. His ancestor might have been born at a time when a man could 'have it all', but those times were gone. There could be no honour in thinking otherwise—not a shred of it.

I have made my choice and I will abide by it. Carla is in the past now, and she must stay there. My future is with Francesca. And Francesca has made her choice too—she has chosen to be my wife.

He walked into his study, sitting himself down at his mahogany desk, ready to catch up on work after several days of entertaining Francesca and her family. His eyes flickered. He had made his choice—Francesca had made hers. But Carla— Carla had not made a choice, had she?

For a moment—just a brief, flashing moment before that guillotine cut down again across his mind—he saw her that final morning.

Naked, stripped bare of everything that she'd thought she had—everything she had presumed.

The guillotine sliced down. Harsh thoughts

sliced down with it. It was a harshness that was necessary. Essential. And not just for Carla.

Well, she should not have presumed! He had given her no cause to do so—none! He could acquit himself of that! He had never—not once—given her to think otherwise! And she hadn't needed any such reminder from him! She'd said she'd always known, always accepted the necessary limitations of their time together. That it would be…could only be…for a fixed duration.

To our time together.

That had been his very first toast to her. Right from the outset. And their time together had now ended. That was all there was to it.

Impatiently, ruthlessly, he switched on his computer. It fired up and he flicked to the Internet to check his emails. The home page of a leading financial newspaper sprang up, and there, in lead story position, was a headline that stilled him totally.

He had made his choice, Francesca had made *her* choice, and now it seemed that Carla Charteris, after all, was making hers…

Marriage merger keeps Viscari Hotels in the family—Falcone's ambitions thwarted!

He stared, seeing the headline. Seeing the photo that went with it.

Feeling the jagged emotion, like a serrated blade, knifing into him.

The sonorous music swelled, lifting upwards to one last crescendo before falling silent. The hushed murmurings of the congregation stilled as the priest raised his hands and began to speak the words of the ancient sacrament in the age-old ceremony.

Inside her breast Carla could feel her heart beating like a hammer. Crushing all compunction about what she was doing—what she was making Vito do so bitterly against his will.

Emotion filled her and she felt a low, fine tremble go through her, as if her whole being were about to shatter as she stood there, gowned in white, her face veiled. Stood beside the man who was her bridegroom. Waiting for him to say the words that would unite them in marriage.

That would free her, finally, from the hell in which she lived.

But there were no words. There was only silence.

At her side, Vito stood immobile. He had not touched her since she'd walked stiffly down the aisle, her back aching with tension—tension that had kept her in hell for weeks now. A hell she had dragged Vito into as well.

But she didn't care—could not care. Could only keep going with the desperate remedy her mother had offered her—a remedy that was, she knew with the last fragment of her sane mind, poisoning her.

She *would not* let Vito go. She could not— *dared* not. If she let him go she would plunge down into the abyss. She *had* to marry him—she just had to! She would not be safe until she did. Safe from everything that was devouring her.

When I'm married to him I can be safe! I can be Signora Viscari and have a role to play, a person to be. Being his wife will give me protection.

Her mother thought it was only protection from the sneers of the world, the gossip and the jibes, that she wanted, but that was not the protection that she so desperately sought. She needed protection from herself.

Without Vito's ring keeping me safe, keeping me here in Rome, keeping my days spent organising my wedding, without all that I'd be terrified...terrified...

Cold snaked down her back. It was terror—the absolute terror that possessed her.

That she'd go to Cesare and beg him...beg him...

Beg him to take her back on any terms—any terms at all!

In her vision she saw again that damnable triptych—the lordly Conte flanked by his pure, perfect wife...and his lowly mistress.

Her stomach hollowed. Once she had thought herself far above comparing herself to the Caradino beauty. In this day and age there could be no such role for any woman. None.

How desperately wrong she had been.

Love makes slaves of us. Strips everything from us. Craves only the object of our heart...

She felt herself tremble again as she stood beside Vito, waiting for him to say the words that would keep her safe. Safe from all that tore at her.

Her mother's cruel description seared in her head. 'Cesare's mistress', she'd called her daughter. And there had been more words too...

'No happy ending.'

Except for Cesare. Cesare with his beautiful, clever, aristocratic bride—the perfect Contessa.

'Do you love her?'

The agonising question she'd hurled at him haunted her, seared in her head now, as she stood rigid with tension beside the man she was forcing to marry her.

And in her head Cesare's reply came again.

'Love is an irrelevance.'

Her face convulsed beneath her veil. Words tumbled through her head, hectic and desperate.

And it will be irrelevant for me too! I don't love Vito, and his emotion for me is only loathing and bitter hatred for what I've done to him, for the price I'm making him pay to get his family shares back. But when I'm safe—truly safe—I can let him go. In six months...a year...he can get on with his life again. I'll ask for an annul-

ment and release Vito and then he can go and find that blonde of his if he really wants to. He can have it all—the shares, the blonde, everything... It won't be the end of the world for him, for her. They can sort it out between them if they really want to.

As for herself—well, this time around it would be *her* choice not to be married! *She* would be the one to end it!

I'll walk out with my head held high—no one will pity me! No one will think me scorned ever again! And Cesare and his beautiful, nobly born, terrifyingly clever, oh-so-damn-wonderful bride can go on having their wonderful life together and I won't care—I won't! I'll have shown him that I can do very well without him! That I've survived.

As if surfacing from a deep, suffocating dive, she became aware that the silence was lengthening. That Vito was still not saying the words she needed to hear—the words that would rescue her from this hell she was in.

Her head jerked towards him, her eyes distending. Filling with urgency.

Then finally Vito was speaking. But it was not to the priest. It was to her. His face stark, he was turning towards her. Saying words that drained the air from her lungs.

'I won't do this, Carla.'

She heard his words. But they came from a long, long way away. There was a roaring in her head…

'No, Mum—I said *no*!'

Carla's voice was like a knife. Her mother was arguing with her, trying to make her go back to Guido's villa with her. But she could not bear another moment of her mother's company.

Raging, shouting, almost hysterical, Carla sat in the vestry, on a hard bench, her nails digging into her palms.

'I'm going back to my apartment.'

How she'd got there she could not remember—one of the wedding cars, she supposed, waiting by the rear entrance to the church, had taken her away from the avid, buzzing speculation of the congregation. But now she was finally there in her bedroom, standing in her wedding dress.

Palest white, like the decor in her apartment. As if she might disappear into it…

A bead of hysteria bubbled in her throat. She fought it down. She must not let it out. She must keep it deep inside her. Must, instead, reach behind her back and with stiff, aching arms undo, hook by hook, the gown she had put on less than three hours ago at Guido's house.

I was so nearly safe—so nearly! And now…

She felt terror beat up in her—had to fight it down. Fight down the cold, sick feeling inside her that was running in every vein like liquid nitrogen.

He jilted me. Vito jilted me. Turned me down. Rejected me. Refused to marry me… Refused, refused, refused…

She felt the hysteria in her throat again, felt her eyes distend, felt pressure in her head as if it might explode. Felt her fingers tremble as the last of the hooks were undone and the heavy, beaded satin and lace gown plummeted to the floor.

She stepped out of it, twisted out of her shoes. God knew where her veil was—she'd torn it from her as she'd gained the vestry, with Vito's arm clamped around hers. If it hadn't been she'd have fainted on the spot. As it was she'd swayed, felt the church whirling around her, and heard a choking noise come from her throat.

She could be glad of that—glad that it had given her a lie to cling to.

'The bride is indisposed...'

Hysteria clawed again. Yes, 'indisposed'—that was what she was.

Not jilted, not rejected, not spurned.

Somewhere in the depths of her head she knew, with a kind of piercing pain, that she had only got what she deserved.

I forced Vito to the altar—behaved shamefully...selfishly.

Desperately.

She walked into the bathroom, yanking on the shower. She stepped under the plunging water, still in her underwear, her hair still pinned into its elaborate coiffeur, soaking herself in the hot, punishing water.

How long she stood there, she could not say. She knew only that it seemed to take an agony of time to peel off the underwear clinging to her streaming wet body—to free herself from the silken mesh of her stockings, push down her panties, yank off her bra, until she was standing there, a mess of lingerie in the shower tray, her hair covering her face, her back, standing there in the scorching hot water, shivering violently...

With shaking hands she turned the water off, pushed the dripping locks from her face, clambered out of the cubicle to seize a towel for her hair, for her body, her feet. She was still shaking, though her skin was red and overheated.

Somehow she made it to her bed. Somehow she thrust the wet towels from her, crawled under the covers like a wounded animal. Somehow, she curled her body, knees drawn up, arms wrapped about herself, her still wet hair damp on the pillow.

She felt the world recede and the blessed mercy of sleep came over her. The oblivion she sought.

CHAPTER NINE

CESARE SMILED AT his hostess, greeting her with
a kiss of her hand. He'd flown in from the USA
that morning, back from a visit to Francesca—
his first as her fiancé.

In America, seeing her for several days in her
work environment, as opposed to seeing her as
his guest with her family at the Castello Mantegna, she had seemed very…well, *American*…

There, she was not Donna Francesca, she was
Dr Fran Ristori—the aristocratic honorific *'delle'*
had been abandoned, he noticed—and she was
clearly completely at home in the high-altitude
intellectual freemasonry of her colleagues.

The conversation at the dinner party she'd
given for him at her apartment on campus, to
introduce him to her colleagues, had been virtu-
ally incomprehensible to him, excellent though

his English was. It was his ignorance of astrophysics that had let him down...

But seeing her with her academic colleagues, speaking English with an American accent, so at home in the rarefied atmosphere of her subject, had made him think to ask her again if she were sure of her decision to marry him.

Had she hesitated? If she had, then her words had only negated that hesitation.

'Yes. You've assured me I can be both a *dottore di fisica* and Contessa di Mantegna. That was what I needed to hear. But...' Her clear blue eyes had rested on him. 'What of you, Ces?' She'd paused minutely, then spoken again. 'My spies tell me my arrival was something of an...an interruption for you.'

For the space of a heartbeat he had been silent. Then he had answered. 'What was interrupted is over, Francesca. Be very sure of that.'

Her eyes rested on him again. 'And are *you*?' she'd asked quietly. 'Are you very sure?'

He had felt the beat of his heart, the pulse of his blood. How many beats? Two? Three? More?

Enough for him to exert the necessary control to say what he must.

'Yes,' he had answered. 'She is marrying someone else. I wish her well.'

In his head he had felt the serration of that same knife that had stabbed him when he'd learnt of Carla's engagement to Vito Viscari. He'd remembered the jab he'd felt that last night at the restaurant with Carla, when he'd heard that note of affection for her step-cousin in her voice.

Is that why she's marrying Viscari—just as I am marrying Francesca? An old affection, born of long years of familiarity? A marriage of mutual convenience for them both?

So how could he object? What justification was there for that knife blade slicing into his head as he told Francesca he wished her well? He would not permit it to be there. It served no function and had no cause. No justification. No place in his life. Just as Carla now had no place in his life.

Slowly, Francesca had inclined her head. Then, with a little breath, she had changed the subject. Asked him something anodyne about his flight the next day.

Now, back in Rome, he was attending an evening party, accepting felicitations from friends and social acquaintances. His hostess, he realised with a slight frown, was Estella Farese, who had been present at the restaurant he'd first taken Carla to at the end of the previous summer.

The guillotine sliced down in his mind. He would *not* remember his time with Carla. Would banish it from his memory. Banish everything about it. Looking back was…irrelevant. Choices had been made, decisions taken. Irrevocable decisions—and not just for himself. Carla, too, had made decisions.

Is she married already? Viscari would not have wanted any delay—would have wanted to get those shares safe in his hands as soon as he could.

And that was good, wasn't it? Good that Carla had moved on. And if she'd decided to marry her step-cousin, with his film star looks let alone the fact that he came with a luxury hotel chain—to which *she* was contributing half shareholding—well, that only made Vito Viscari an entirely suitable man for her to marry. Entirely suitable.

So there was no reason—no *good* reason—why he should object to her marriage. Why his jaw should tighten, his eyes harden. Why that same spike of jagged emotion—that serrated blade—should flash across his mind, knifing into him now, as it had when Francesca had put her loaded question to him. The question she had had every right to ask and that he'd had every obligation to answer in the way he had. No valid reason at all. Except…

Except that when I think of her and Viscari—of her and any other man—I want to find her... find her and—

His hostess's voice cut across his thoughts as that serrated blade knifed into him again.

'*Cesare!* How lovely of you to be here!' Estella's greeting was warm. 'Now, do come and tell me—how is dear, *dear* Francesca! *How* delighted I am that you two are finally engaged! We've all had to wait *so* long! *Such* a brilliant young woman.'

She took Cesare's arm, guiding him towards the far side of the salon.

They passed a knot of women, avidly conversing with each other, and they suddenly paused, as if taken aback by his proximity, only continuing as he passed by. Their eager tones, though, penetrated his awareness.

'Jilted! Yes, my dear, I was there! I saw it all! He refused to marry her!'

A titter of unkind laughter followed.

'He wanted the shares, but not the stepdaughter!'

Another voice intervened. 'No, no, it was *she* who balked! She nearly fainted at the altar. He almost had to carry her away. It's my belief...'

The voice dropped, but not so low that it did not reach Cesare's ears.

'...that she couldn't accept Viscari when she might have had—' She broke off.

The first voice came again—spiteful and contemptuous. 'She never had a *chance* of that! How could she? Mantegna has been promised to the delle Ristori girl all his life! Just as their engagement now proves!'

Estella sailed on by, speaking a little louder than she needed to, as if to drown out the gossips' voices. She proceeded to quiz him about his trip to America, about the forthcoming wedding, about whether Francesca would continue with her research career afterwards.

Cesare felt himself go into automatic mode, giving responses almost at random. But inside his head a bomb was exploding in devastating slow motion.

She didn't marry him.

The words repeated in his head. Like a gunshot.

She didn't marry him.

They stayed in his head for the duration of the evening. Were still there as he left, exhausted by polite enquiries after Francesca, and how the wedding preparations were proceeding, and showers of felicitations and congratulations and well-wishing.

There had been no further tactless or untoward remarks about what was clearly sending the gossips into overdrive.

A jilting at the altar! A fainting bride! A mother in hysterics. *Two* mothers in hysterics! And all of Rome to witness it!

Back in his apartment, the words were still there, ricocheting around inside his skull. He strode across the room, pulled open the drinks cabinet. Fetching a bottle of whisky, he poured a hefty slug. He knocked it back in one.

She didn't marry him.

Then, with a rasp, he pushed the whisky bottle away, relocked the cabinet. He went into the room he reserved for his office. He needed distraction. He would check on his affairs.

Grimly, he turned on his PC, letting it fire up. So what if she didn't marry Viscari? What was it to him? Nothing—nothing at all! *She* was nothing to him! He'd made his decision—put her aside. Finished the affair. *Finished it!*

He'd had no choice to do otherwise. No choice at all.

I could not have them both—those times are gone.

His mouth contorted and he rubbed his hand across his face—a rough gesture, as if he could wipe out what was inside his head.

Two images formed in his vision.

Francesca delle Ristori—the woman he was going to marry.

Carla Charteris—the woman he had put aside to do so.

Carla...

And, like a sluice gate opening, a dam breaking, all the images that he had kept out of his head since the moment he'd walked out of her apartment stormed in upon him.

More than images...worse than images.

Memories—vivid, tangible, indelible.

Carla swimming with him at midnight in the pool at the villa in Lazio, their naked bodies glistening in starlight.

Carla, her limbs wound with his, spine arched as she cried out in his arms.

Carla smiling at him across the dinner table, telling him something about Luciezo, or Tintoretto, or Michelangelo—some detail of art history he did not know—while he set it in historical context and they discussed the implications of it.

Carla shaking her hair free as he drove along the autostrada *towards the villa in Lazio, taking their time off together, looking forward to noth-*

ing more than easy, restful, peaceable days together—to sensual, passion-fuelled nights...

Memory after memory.

Nothing more than memory now. Now and for ever—for the rest of his life.

As it must be.

Desperately, urgently, he made his thoughts fly across the ocean, back to where he'd left the woman who was going to be his *contessa*, his destined bride, the woman who was right for him in every way. But Francesca's image would not come—would not be conjured. Instead dark hair, blue-violet eyes, that rich, sensuous mouth that could smile, or kiss, or gasp in passion at its peak...all occluded his vision.

She didn't marry him.

The words came again—sinuous now, soft and dulcet, weaving in and out of his synapses. He felt his blood quicken, let memory ripen in his thoughts.

More than memory.

He shifted restlessly in his chair. It had been so long...so long since he had set her aside. Yet she was here—so close. Across the city—a kilometre or two…no more than that. How often had he gone to her apartment in those six months that had been their time together? How often had his hands closed over her shoulders, drawing her lush body to his as his mouth lowered to her parting lips, tasting the delectable sensual nectar of her kiss, deepening to heated arousal…?

Carla—with her blue-violet eyes, her rich mouth, her full breasts and rounded hips—with the dark, lustrous hair he'd loved to spear and tangle his hands in as he spread her body out on the bed for himself to caress, possess…to take and be taken while flames of passion had seared them both—Carla… Ah, Carla, who was only a dozen rooftops away…

Carla, whom he had set aside to fulfil his responsibilities to his name, his house… Carla, who could never be more to him than what she had been—and to have been that was…

Carla, who had thought to marry a man who was nothing to her! Merely for the reallocation of a handful of shares.

His mouth twisted. He had told himself she was entirely entitled to marry Viscari, had made himself applaud it—be glad of it. Glad that he could set her aside knowing she would be making a future for herself as her step-cousin's wife. Telling himself that her marriage made sense, was entirely suitable—just as his own was.

He could tell himself all he liked.

It was a lie. A barefaced lie to hide the truth of why she had taken such a step.

That was not why she'd walked up the aisle towards Vito Viscari! She'd done it for one reason and one reason only and he knew it—knew it with every burning fibre of his being.

She did it to punish me—because of what I did to her. Because I put her aside...put her out of my life.

That was the reason—the only reason.

Emotion reared up in him—savage, powerful. Fuelling the memories surging through his head. Impelling him from the room, from the apartment.

To one destination only.

Carla swayed, her body racked with pain. Her mind more so. Twenty-four hours—had it really been only twenty-four hours? Twenty-four hours since she had collapsed into the blessed oblivion that had blotted out the horrors of the afternoon before?

She clenched her hands, feeling her painted nails digging into her palms. She welcomed the pain. She deserved it. Deserved it for being the cretinous, contemptible fool that she had been.

To think I could get him to marry me! To salve my shattered pride! To let me outstare the world—outstare the man who threw me aside as if I was less than nothing to him!

Mortification filled her—and self-contempt. And bitter, bitter remorse.

She deserved what Vito had done to her. Deserved his refusal to be blackmailed into saving her stupid, stupid face. Deserved everything.

She trailed into the kitchen, filled the kettle. She would drink tea and force herself to eat, despite the sickness in her stomach.

The future stretched ahead of her—empty and bleak.

She would leave Rome. She must. And her mother would be leaving too. No doors would be open to her now—Lucia Viscari would ensure that. For who would receive a woman who had sold her own husband's legacy—half the entire company—to his business rival, just to punish the man who had jilted her daughter at the altar? No, Marlene would leave for Spain and she would go with her. What else could she do?

The doorbell jangled, making her start. Dear God, not her mother again, surely? She had left only a few hours earlier, her fury at Vito's behaviour venomous, her vengeance upon him ruthless.

Carla had tried to stop her.

'Do you blame him, Mum? *Do* you? I behaved despicably to him! None of this was his fault, and yet I made him take the fall for it! And if you sell those shares to Nic Falcone you will have behaved as badly! Sell them to Vito—like he's implored you to do ever since Guido died!'

But Marlene had been deaf to Carla's pleas. Driven by maternal rage at her daughter's humiliation. There had been nothing Carla could do.

The doorbell came again—insistent now.

She put the kettle down, trailed to the door. Opened it.

Cesare walked in.

Shock, like a seismic wave in slow motion, detonated within Carla, hollowing her out, draining the breath from her body. Faintness drummed at her and she clung to the door frame for support.

He took it from her, closed it. Turned to her.

There was a blaze in his eyes. A black fire.

'Get out.' Her voice was faint, and very far away.

He ignored her, walked past her into her sitting room. His eyes came back to her as she stepped inside. She clutched her dressing gown to her, as if it might support her.

'I said get out,' she said again.

He looked at her. That black fire was still in his eyes. 'Were you really going to marry him? Did you truly intend to go through with it?'

'Yes!' she answered, her voice a searing hiss.

Emotion was knifing inside her. To see Cesare *here*, in her apartment, a handful of metres away from her…

His mouth tightened like the line of a whip. 'They can't decide, the gossips, quite what happened yesterday. Whether he threw *you* over or you him.' He paused. 'So which was it?'

She gave a laugh. A savage, vicious laugh.

'Which do you think, Cesare?' Her face convulsed. 'I should be used to it, shouldn't I? Being thrown aside!'

She took a shuddering breath. Lifting her chin, her eyes flashing like daggers, she clutched the material of her robe across her breasts, as if keeping him at bay. But she didn't need to keep him at bay, did she? He didn't want her...he would never want her again.

She slashed a hand through the air. 'So get out, Cesare! Get out of my apartment and out of my life—just *get out*!'

He stood motionless while she hurled her diatribe at him. Then, when all the fury of her words was spent, he stepped towards her.

'Get out...' she said again. Her voice was hoarse.

She should move...she should retreat. Flee. Barricade herself in her bedroom.

She could not move.

'You should not have tried to marry him,' said Cesare. His voice was strange.

There was a choking sound from her throat, but she had no words to answer him. He did not need any.

'When I saw that photo of you, that announcement in the financial press, I—' He stopped. Could not continue.

Emotion welled in him. Dark and blackening. Somewhere, far across the Atlantic Ocean, was the woman he was supposed to marry. While here…

'You should not have tried to marry him,' he said again.

From the depths of his mind he tried to conjure Francesca's face. But she was not there. He tried to say her name in his head, but he could not. That guillotine had descended across his mind, cutting him in half. There was a woman's name he needed to say—

The name of the woman who stood before him.

Her eyes were huge in her face, her hands convulsing on the silk of her robe. A robe he knew well. Raw silk, peacock-blue, shot with violet like her eyes. He'd said as much to her once as he'd slid it from her naked body, letting it pool on the floor.

He stepped towards her, reaching out his hand for the shoulder of her robe, letting his fingers slide over its silken surface. He felt her body shudder beneath his touch. Saw her close her eyes as if to shut him out, her long lashes wet.

'Carla...'

He said her name—the name he needed to say. Felt his hand fasten on her shoulder, his other hand graze down the edge of the material across her collarbone. Her delicate, intricate collarbone... The pale satin skin below yielded to his touch. And only to his.

No one else's! No other man should touch her.

His blood pulsed like a hammer in his veins. He could not do without her. Not tonight.

Memory drummed across his mind. *This* was why he was here. To make those memories real again.

He lifted her chin, cupping it with his fingers. Her eyes flared open. There was terror in them— and more than terror.

'Don't do this…' Her voice was faint.

He shook his head. 'Then tell me to go,' he said. 'You've said it to me over and over again. Say it to me now. Say it, Carla—tell me to go. To get out of your life.'

She could not speak. Could only stare.

'Tell me to get out, Carla.'

His voice was a harsh, raw husk, his mouth twisting as he spoke, his eyes spearing hers. A pulse throbbed at his throat and his long fingers plunged into her hair, indenting into her skull. Holding her for himself…*only* for himself…

'Tell me to get out,' he said again, one final time.

But she could not. She could do nothing. Nothing at all. Could only feel her lips part, helpless, hopeless as, with a rasp deep in his throat, he lowered his mouth to hers, grazing it, taking his fill.

'I want one last time,' he said, his voice still a husk, his eyes still burning with that black fire. 'One last time, Carla. One last time to show you why you should not have agreed to marry another man. *Any* other man—'

He grazed her mouth with his again, his hand slipping the silk from her shoulder, exposing a single breast.

'So tell me to go, Carla…or tell me to stay…or tell me nothing at all.' His hand moved, to cup the lush curve of her breast, so rich and ripe, to feel its crest peak and bloom within his palm,

And then the time for speaking was done. With a surge of his blood, he opened her mouth beneath his, his hand tightening at her breast, kneading the soft, aroused flesh.

A moan escaped her throat. Helpless. Hopeless. She could not speak, could not protest. She could do only what every part of her body, her being, wanted…craved her to do.

Her hands snaked around his back, hauling him to her, crushing his hips into the cradle of her body, feeling her body surge, his body answer hers.

And then the black fire took them both…

Carla moved slowly, as if emerging from paralysis. Consciousness seeped through her. For a moment she lay there, motionless. At her side, his limbs heavy upon her, Cesare slept. His face was in repose, and for a long, timeless moment Carla looked upon it.

Behind her eyes, thoughts ran.

There was a sickness inside her.

Slowly, infinitely slowly, she began to move. He did not stir. Weak with gratitude for that one small mercy, she slid from the bed. Silently, desperately, she found clothes, crept from the bedroom, forced unwilling limbs into them, found her handbag, her keys.

The morning light was dim—dawn barely broken. Her heart was pounding…the sickness was overwhelming her. She stepped forward, as if impelled by a power she could not resist.

At the door of the bedroom she halted. Her eyes, stricken, went to the figure lying in her bed, sprawled across it, the strong planes of his muscled back delineated in the dawn light. Emotion, like a wolf, leapt in her throat to devour her. Her hand was pressed to her mouth, and a sound that might have been a sob was stifled before it could be born.

Then, as if it required all the strength in her body, she turned away.

Left the apartment.

Left the city.

Fled for her very life.

CHAPTER TEN

THE SPANISH SUN was warm on Carla's bare arms and legs as she sat on the terrace of her mother's huge, newly purchased villa on this most exclusive stretch of the Costas. It seemed a lifetime ago since she had been in Rome. Yet only a handful of months had passed since she'd fled like a wounded creature.

A haunted expression filled her eyes. Then, deliberately, she picked up the newspaper at her side, turning, as she often did now, to the financial pages.

Her expression tensed. Yes, there was another news item—small, but immediately eye-catching to her—about Viscari Hotels. Something about yet another fraught board meeting, now that Nic Falcone was co-owner of the whole company and helping himself to the pick of Viscari

Hotels across the world, dismembering Vito's inheritance piecemeal.

Guilt, familiar and shaming, fused through Carla. Guilt and remorse.

How could I have done that to him? How could I?

But she knew how—knew, even as the hot Spanish sun beat down on her, how her whole being had writhed in the torment of Cesare's rejection of her, in the humiliation of knowing that she had only been exactly what her mother had feared she was.

Nothing better than his mistress. To be set aside the moment his aristocratic bride beckoned!

She closed her eyes, fighting the emotion that swept up in her. What good was it to remember? Cesare had treated her by his own rules—and it had been she who had been the fool! A fool to fall in love with him—a fool ever to think she could have her happy ending…that Cesare could return her love for him…

She felt her stomach churn again. And the worst fool of all to have let him into her apartment that last, disastrous, fatal night after Vito's jilting of her. Fool upon fool!

And now…

Her hand dropped the newspaper, slid across her stomach to ease the nausea that bit there.

Dear God, how great a fool she was!

'Carla, darling, there you are!'

Her mother's voice was a welcome distraction as Marlene emerged out of the villa. She paused, surveying her daughter.

'How are you feeling this morning?' she asked carefully.

Carla stood up. 'I'm OK, Mum.'

'*Are* you?' Marlene's eyes worked over her, concern in their expression.

She was about to say more, Carla could tell, and she needed to stop her. She picked up the newspaper.

'There's another piece in here about Viscari and Falcone,' she said.

There was reproof in her voice, and she could see her mother's colour heighten.

She held up a hand. 'Mum, don't say anything—we're never going to agree on this. But

I did treat Vito appallingly.' She took a breath, saying what she had resolved. 'I'm going to go to Rome. I have to see him—to…apologise. And also,' she carried on, still not letting her mother speak, 'I want to put my apartment on the market.' She paused. 'I'm never going to live in Italy again, so there is no point owning it. And besides—'

She halted. She would not tell her mother that she intended to do more than merely apologise to Vito. Since her mother had profited hugely from selling Guido's shares to Vito's rival, she would make what amends she could by gifting the proceeds from the sale of her flat—bought, after all, with Guido's legacy to her—to Vito. He could use it to help fund his financial recovery. Pittance though it was, it was the only thing she could think of doing.

'Darling…' Her mother's voice was openly worried. 'Are you sure you want to go back to Rome? I mean—'

Carla shook her head. 'No, I don't want to—but I must.'

* * *

It was what she'd kept repeating to herself—right up to the grim moment when she bearded Vito in his office in Rome.

The ordeal was gruelling. From the moment she arrived she could feel eyes on her—curious…openly hostile.

Vito himself was stone-faced as she made her stumbling, tight-throated expression of her remorse.

'I'm desperately sorry, Vito, and deeply ashamed of myself. I let my own misery over Cesare consume me. It made me behave vilely to you—and…' she swallowed '…to…to your girlfriend.' She paused again, uncomfortable. 'I hope… I hope you were able to make it up with her after… well…since then.'

A bleak look passed across his face. 'That wasn't possible,' he said.

Carla felt guilt bite at her again. 'I'm sorry,' she said. 'Would…would it help if I…if I went to see her? Apologised for what I said…what I did?'

The bleak look came again. 'I have no idea

where Eloise is. She's vanished. I've been trying to find her since—' It was his turn to break off.

'Oh, Vito, I'm sorry!'

Carla's voice was even more apologetic, her guilt ever deeper. There had been something in her step-cousin's voice that she recognised in her-self—a bleakness that matched her own.

Her face twisted. 'I didn't realise she was so important to you... I mean, you usually—' She broke off again.

Vito looked at her, his eyes strained. 'Yes, I know. I *do* usually have some long-legged blonde on my arm,' he said, echoing the words she'd used. 'But Eloise—'

He broke off again, and now Carla *knew* she could see something in his drawn face that she recognised only too well. Vito's dark eyes looked at her with a nakedness in them that smote her.

'Eloise was different. I wanted so much to spend time with her—to discover if...if she was the one woman I'd ever met whom I could—'

He broke off again.

'And now I'll never know,' he said.

The bleakness in his voice broke Carla. Impulsively she stepped forward.

'Vito—let me help! Please let me help you find her. There must be a way—there *must*!'

He looked at her. 'How? She won't answer my texts or my calls. I don't have any address for her in London, where she lives, because she works as a nanny. I've had investigators checking nanny agencies, but nothing—absolutely *nothing*! She's vanished!'

Frustration and pain were clear in his voice. Carla felt her mind racing. An idea was forming in her mind.

'Vito—listen. Even if *you* can't find her—and neither can your investigators—maybe…maybe the press can!'

Vito looked at her blankly. Carla felt words tumble from her in her desperation to make amends—any kind of amends—to the stepcousin she had treated so shamefully.

'Vito, I'm a journalist—I know how the press works. What about this? I'm fairly friendly with the features editor on one of those glossy international celebrity magazines. She loves it that I know loads of the people she likes to put in it, especially you! I've always been very discreet, but this time—'

Swiftly she outlined her idea.

Vito looked at her. For the first time the lines around his eyes seemed to lighten. 'Do you think it has a chance?' he asked.

Carla looked at him. 'It's worth a shot, isn't it? A centre spread of you, with a glamorously romantic photo of you both, and a headline asking, *"Can you find my beautiful Eloise?"* Those glossy celebrity magazines have a *huge* readership!'

'Can you set it up for me? A meeting with this features editor?' There was sudden urgency in Vito's voice.

Carla smiled. The first time she'd smiled for a long time. If this was some way to make amends to Vito, however belated, she would do it.

'I'll phone her now,' she said.

Five minutes later she put the phone back on Vito's desk.

'She almost bit my hand off,' she told him.

She could see her step-cousin's eyes flare—fill with hope.

He got to his feet, came round to her. Took her hands. 'Thank you,' he said.

Emotion welled up in her. 'Oh, Vito, don't thank me! Not after what I did to you! I can never forgive myself—*never*! I was just so…so twisted up inside. So—'

She broke off again. Half turned away. But Vito did not let her go. Instead he put his arms around her, hugged her tightly. She felt tears prick at her eyes.

Then, abruptly, Vito stood back from her, looked at her with shock in his face.

'Carla—' There was disbelief in his voice.

Too late, she realised why. She stepped away, disengaging her hands.

'Cesare?' Vito's voice was hollow.

Colour stained her cheekbones. 'After…after you refused to marry me he…he turned up at my apartment. It was—'

'Does he *know*?' There was a steely note in Vito's voice.

Violently, Carla shook her head. 'No! And he mustn't! Vito—he *mustn't*!'

Vito's brows snapped together, giving him a quelling appearance. 'He must know *at once*!' he retorted. 'Before he goes any further with his engagement!'

Carla caught at his sleeve. 'No! Please, Vito! I couldn't bear it!' There was panic in her face.

For a moment his quelling expression held. Then, abruptly, it vanished.

'I understand,' he said. His voice changed. 'Carla, look…now that we've made our peace with each other I think we should show Rome that the family rift…is no more.'

He held up his hand decisively. 'I know that the gossips couldn't decide just why our wedding never took place, but I want to show them that whatever has happened since—' he did not spell out what her mother had done '—you and I, at least, are friends. So I think we should be seen out socially, while you're here in Rome, to confirm that.'

She looked at him uncertainly. 'If…if you want,' she said.

How could she refuse anything that Vito asked of her, given how badly she had treated him? Socialising in Rome might be the most gruelling ordeal she could imagine right now, but she must face it for Vito's sake.

And if I fear I might see Cesare—well, why should I? Viscari circles don't usually overlap with his, and anyway Cesare's probably in his castello *planning his wedding...*

She felt the nausea bite again—and something worse than nausea. Much, much worse.

'Good.' Vito nodded. He smiled. 'How about tonight?'

She paled. 'Tonight?' she echoed faintly.

Vito quirked an eyebrow. 'You have something more pressing?'

Slowly she shook her head, realised that in all conscience she could not refuse.

That evening, as she stood staring blankly at her reflection in the mirror, she knew the last thing she wanted was to go out into society—even though she owed it to Vito. So, ignoring the knots in her stomach, she threw one last glance at herself, reassured by the dark indigo evening gown, generously cut—nothing clinging or curvaceous now—and her immaculate hair and make-up.

Her phone buzzed to tell her that Vito was waiting for her in his car below, and she left her apartment.

She had spent the afternoon with estate agents and her solicitor, booking a removal company to transfer her possessions to her mother's house. She would tell Vito this evening that she was going to hand him the proceeds of the sale—it wasn't much, compared to the loss he'd suffered, thanks to her mother, but it was all she could do.

She paid little attention to where he was taking her, but as they walked inside an ornate *palazzo*, the venue for the fundraising reception for a *museo di antiquity* that Vito was attending, she suddenly froze.

Her hand clawed on Vito's sleeve. 'This is the Palazzo Mantegna!'

He glanced at her. 'I know,' he said. 'That's why I brought you here—Cesare will be here as one of the *museo*'s patrons.'

Desperately, Carla tried to pull away.

But Vito's hand clamped over hers. 'Carla—he has to know. He *has* to!'

A drumming filled her senses.

Cesare was talking to his fellow *museo* patrons, but for all his polite conversation he had no inclination to be there. His mood was grim.

Francesca was still in America, vacating her apartment, making ready to move back to Italy and become his *contessa*. He was glad of her absence. How could he face her after what he had done? Committing an act of folly so extreme he could not now believe that he had done it.

Folly? Was that what it had been? That final, self-indulgent, devil-driven night with Carla? The sour taste of self-disgust filled him. Of shame.

I went to her with my betrothal ring on Francesca's finger! And yet I presumed to accuse her of being prepared to marry another man! As if she had betrayed me...spurned me for another man.

In that one shameful night he had behaved unforgivably to the woman he'd undertaken to marry *and* the one whom he could never marry.

Could never again possess. Could never again see, or have anything to do with.

She is lost to me for ever.

As he said the words, he felt something twist inside him, as if the point of a knife had broken off, stayed in his guts. It would stay there, lodged for ever. Scar tissue would grow around it, but it would remain for all his life. A wound that would not heal…

'Signor Conte—'

He was being called to the podium to make a short speech. The moment he'd done that he'd leave. Tomorrow he'd head back to his *castello* and ready it for his future bride.

He felt his mind veer away. Contemplating his wedding—his bride—was not what he wanted to do. Memory sifted in his mind. It had been a function similar to this—the opening of that exhibition he'd lent the triptych to—where he'd first had his interest caught by Carla Charteris.

He could see her now instantly, in his mind's eye, her figure sheathed in that cobalt blue cocktail dress, her svelte brunette beauty immediately firing his senses. Calling to him…

His gaze flickered blankly over the throng of guests milling around in the palatial hall of his ancestors' former residence in Rome.

Flickered—and stilled.

No—he was imagining it. He *must* be. It could not be—

Without volition he was walking forward. Striding. People were stepping aside for him.

She had seen him. He saw it in her paling face, her distended eyes. Her hand was clutching at the sleeve of the man with her.

Viscari! With an inner snarl that came from some deep, primitive part of him, Cesare felt jealous rage spear up inside him as he reached the couple.

He could see Vito Viscari step forward slightly, as if to shelter Carla, whose face was still bleached and stark. Then, with a little breathless sigh, she started to crumple.

There were voices—deep and masculine, angry and agitated—penetrating her brain. Her eyelids flickered feebly, and she became aware that she was perched dizzily on a chair in a small antechamber—and that Vito and Cesare were standing over her.

'Are you all right?' Cesare's demand was stentorian, his face grim. The question was directed at her—he was ignoring Vito totally.

But it was Vito who was answering for her. 'No,' he said tersely, 'she is not.'

Carla's heart was hammering, the blood drumming in her ears.

Cesare's gaze snapped to Vito. 'What is wrong?'

Vito started to speak, but Carla reached for his arm.

'Vito, no! *No!*' Terror was in her now. She had to stop him—she *had* to!

But the expression on Vito's face was one she'd never seen before. Angry—stern. He was squaring up to Cesare, who was glaring at him, his face dark and closed.

Vito's chin lifted. He paid no attention to Carla. 'Your marriage plans are going to have to be altered,' he said to Cesare. 'Carla is pregnant.'

Cesare's car speeded along the *autostrada* heading into the Lazio countryside. At his side, Carla sat silent. Memory was biting like a wolf in her mind. How she had sat beside Cesare like this that first weekend together as he'd sped her towards his beautiful little rococo love nest.

I thought I could handle an affair with Cesare. A civilised, sensual affair, for the mutual enjoyment of both of us.

How utterly, totally wrong she had been. How incomparably stupid. Folly after folly! All compounded by the single greatest folly she had committed.

To have fallen in love with him. Cesare di Mondave, Conte di Mantegna. A man who would never marry her.

Except—and that wolf bit again, in her throat now—now that was exactly what he was prepared to do.

The irony of it was agonising. Unbearable. As unbearable as the words she had heard her stepcousin uttering last night. And Cesare's explosive outburst… Vito's coldly terse assurance.

Both of them had ignored her until a moan had come from her lips, and then suddenly they'd both been there, bending over her.

She'd pushed them both away, struggling upright. Cesare's arm had come around her instantly, but she'd pulled herself free. Her head
had been pounding, her heart racing.

'Leave me alone! Both of you!'

A look had been thrown between Cesare and
Vito. Cesare had said something to Vito she had
not been able to hear, hearing only the grimness
in his voice. Then Vito had nodded.

'Be sure you do,' he'd said, in that same terse
voice.

Then Cesare had looked at Carla. His face had
been unreadable. He'd seemed a thousand miles
away. A million.

'All the necessary arrangements will be made,'
he said to her. 'I will fetch you tomorrow. Until
then—'

He'd exchanged one more look with Vito, and
then he had gone. It had been Vito who'd seen
her back to her apartment, talking to her—*at*
her—all the way. She'd said nothing, her mouth
tight, compressed. Right up until Vito had seen
her into her apartment.

Then she'd turned to him. 'I am not marrying Cesare,' she'd said.

Vito had said nothing. And then—'He has given me his word that he will. For now, that is enough.'

He'd left her, and this morning Cesare had arrived. She'd seen his eyes moving around the apartment and had known that he was remembering the fatal night he'd forced his way in, daring her to make him leave.

And now he's reaping the consequences.

She'd wanted to laugh, hysterically, but had silenced herself. Almost wordlessly he'd ushered her down to his waiting car and she'd gone with him, her suitcase packed.

She'd wanted to go back to Spain, to her mother, and yet here she was, in Cesare's car, going back to the place that had once been a place of bliss for her. Now, it was evident, it was going to be the scene where Cesare di Mondave steeled himself to offer to marry his former mistress who'd so disastrously got herself pregnant.

'Is it cool enough for you? I can turn up the air conditioning.'

Cesare's voice interrupted her bleak thoughts. His tone was polite. Distant.

'Perfectly cool, thank you,' she answered, her tone matching his.

He drove on in silence.

At the villa, Lorenzo was there to greet them, as he always had been. Carla was glad of his presence—it insulated her from Cesare.

Yet as lunch was served, and Lorenzo departed, suddenly she was alone with Cesare again. She watched him reach for his wine glass. Then set it down, untouched. He looked across at her from the head of the table to herself at the foot. His face was still expressionless.

It hurt her to see him. Hurt her eyes to take in the features of his face, which had once been so familiar to her—so familiar that she could have run her fingertips over its contours in the dark and known it to be him out of all the men in all the world.

And now it was the face of a stranger. She could not bear it…

But bear it she must. Must bear, too, the words he now spoke to her.

'Would you have told me that you were pregnant had your step-cousin not intervened?' he asked. His words were staccato.

Carla looked at him. 'No,' she said.

Something flashed in his eyes, but all he said was, 'Why not?'

She gave a shrug—the tiniest gesture. 'To what purpose? You were engaged to another woman.' She paused. 'You still are.'

The dark flash came again. 'You must leave it to me to communicate with my…my former fiancée,' he said heavily. His mouth was set. 'You will understand, I am sure, that this will not be easy for her. This situation is nothing of her making and I must do all that I can to make it as comfortable for her as I can.'

She watched him pick up his wine glass again, and this time he drank deeply from it. His unreadable gaze came back to her.

'Once I have spoken to Francesca—and out of courtesy also to her parents—our betrothal will be formally announced. Until that time I would be grateful…' he took a breath '…if you would be…reticent about our engagement.'

Carla did not answer.

He went on. As if he were forcing himself. 'And for the same reason I would ask you to stay here, in the villa, until I am free to become formally betrothed to you.'

Her answer was a silent inclination of her head.

For a long moment Cesare let his gaze rest on her. Emotions were mounting in his chest, but he kept them tightly leashed. It was essential for him to do so. He watched her pick up her knife and fork and start to eat. She did not look pregnant. But then, she was scarcely into her second trimester.

He felt his insides twist and knot.

She carries my child! A child she would never have told me about! I would have married Francesca—had children by her, a son to be my heir—while all along Carla would have been raising another child of mine, born outside marriage.

For a second—just a second—images flashed in his head. His ancestor, Count Alessandro, flanked by the two women in his life. His wife—the mother of his heir—and his mistress, her body rich with his bastard child.

That will not be me! Never.

Inside, he felt his leashed emotions lash him, as if trying to break free, but he only tightened the leash on them. It was not safe to do otherwise. He must ignore them, focus only on the practicalities of what must happen now. His world had just been turned upside down and his task was to deal with it.

Blank out everything else.

Blank out the memories that assailed him of how often he and Carla had retreated here to the villa to have private time together, relaxing away from their work, their busy lives. Private…intimate… Enjoying each other's company, in bed and out. Enjoying their affair.

An affair he had ended because it could no longer continue—because of the commitment he had to make to his family responsibility, to the woman who had expected to marry him all her adult life.

The commitment that now, because of his own insane behaviour the night he'd gone to Carla's apartment, driven by demons he had not known possessed him, he had to set aside. A commitment overridden by a new, all-consuming commitment. To the child Carla was carrying.

Only to the child?

The question was searing in his head, but he must not let it. Not now—not yet.

Once more he yanked at the leash on his emotions, tightening his grip on them, and let his eyes rest on Carla, so pale, so silent.

Across the table she felt Cesare's tense gaze on her. How often had she eaten here with Cesare in the months they'd spent together? Taking their ease—talking, smiling, laughing—their eyes openly entwining with each other, the air of intimacy between them as potent as their glances.

Yet now it was as if they were each encased in ice.

What can we say to each other? What is there to say? How can we ever speak to each other as we once did? Comfortable, companionable...

'Are you well in the pregnancy?' Cesare's words, still staccato, interrupted her bleak, unanswerable questions.

'Perfectly,' she answered, her tone of voice

echoing his. 'Some nausea, but no more than that. It will ease as I go into the next trimester.'

He nodded. 'I'm glad to hear it.' He paused again. 'I'll book an appointment with whatever obstetrician in Rome you choose. And perhaps it would be sensible to book you into a delivery clinic before long.'

'Thank you,' she answered. She tried to think of something else to say, and failed.

'Have you had an ultrasound yet?'

Another stilted question. Only highlighting the strain between them.

She shook her head, answering no just as stiltedly.

'Perhaps we should book one. Are there any other tests that need to be done?'

'I'll speak to the doctor, but it should all be very straightforward.'

He nodded. 'Good.'

Good? The word echoed in Carla's head, mocking her. 'Good' was a million miles from what it was. She felt nausea rising up in her throat and had to fight it down. She had just told Cesare she was coming out of morning sickness, but this nausea didn't come from her body, from her pregnancy.

It came from a source much deeper inside her.

Stolidly, she ate her way through the rest of the meal.

Painstakingly, Cesare kept a limping conversation going, talking about her pregnancy, asking questions she could scarcely answer.

When the meal was over they repaired for coffee to the terrace, underneath a shady parasol, catching the lightly cooling breeze. Out in the beautiful walled garden the sun sparkled off the water in the pool.

'How much exercise can you take?' Cesare asked.

'As much as I like, really. Swimming is the best—especially as I get closer to my due date,' she answered.

Her eyes went to the pool. So did Cesare's.

Is he remembering too? Remembering how we swam stark naked beneath the stars?

Emotion gripped her, like a knife sliding between her ribs.

Without thinking, Carla reached for the silver

coffee jug, pouring black coffee for Cesare as she had done a hundred times before, handing him the delicate porcelain cup and saucer with its silver crested coffee spoon. He sketched a constrained smile of thanks and took it, sitting back in his chair, crossing one long leg over the other.

Absently, he stirred his coffee. Then, abruptly, he looked across at her as she poured hot milk into her own coffee.

'We can make this work, you know, Carla. We just have to…to set our minds to it.' There was resolution in his voice, determination in his expression.

She lifted her cup to her lips, took a sip, then lowered it. She looked across at him. Her eyes were bleak. Negating his resolve.

'How can we?' she said. 'You'd be marrying your mistress. How can that ever work?' Her voice was tight—so tight it must surely snap, like wire under unbearable tension.

'You were never my *"mistress"*!' The words came from him like bullets. Automatic, instinctive. 'Do not paint yourself as such! We had an affair, Carla—a relationship. It was simply that—' He broke off.

She shut her eyes. Took a ragged breath. She would finish for him. Tell the truth that had always been there, right from the start—the truth that was not her fault, nor his, but that had always set the terms of their relationship.

'It was simply that marriage to me was never on the cards for you—and it still doesn't have to be, Cesare! I'm perfectly prepared to stay stashed away in Spain with my mother. I'll never show my face in Rome again! If you want to pay towards the child's upkeep, you're welcome—but I don't need your money. I'll sign any document you like never to make a claim on your estate, or your heirs.'

She fell silent. Breathless. Inside her there seemed to be a knot—a tight, hard knot that was getting tighter and harder every second. She kept her eyes on Cesare. Fixed. Resolute.

I have to say this—I have to do this. He must hear from me that I do not want this marriage.

She felt a crying out in her heart.

Not a marriage like this! Oh, not a marriage like this!

Across her heart a jagged knife seemed to be dragging its serrated blade. Had she ever had such insanely impossible hopes that he might be falling in love with her? That last evening of their affair, when he'd been so different, she'd thought—dear God, she'd really, truly thought—it might be because he was recognising what she had come to mean to him!

The jagged knife drew her heart's blood from her. But now all she was to him was a burden. An obligation. A duty he must fulfil.

For a moment—an instant—she thought she saw emotion flash darkly across his face. Then it was shuttered.

'That is out of the question,' he said.

He drank his coffee, jerkily lifting the cup to his lips, precisely setting it back down, as if every muscle were under tight control.

He looked across at her. 'Once,' he said, 'it might have been acceptable to have a…a second family, an informal arrangement.'

Into his head flashed that Caradino portrait of

Count Alessandro's mistress, the mother of his illegitimate children, her swollen belly. He thrust the image from his head.

'But that is out of the question these days!' His voice was a snap—a lock to shut out any other possibility.

It did not silence Carla. Her violet eyes flared with emotion. 'It's just the opposite!' she retorted. 'There is no longer any social opprobrium in having children outside marriage. We don't have to go through a marriage ceremony just for appearance's sake! Not like—'

She broke off. A crushing sense of fatalism paralysed her. Words, unsaid, scars inside her head, played themselves silently.

Not like my parents had to...

Cesare's shuttered expression did not change. 'No child of mine will be born outside marriage,' he said.

There were lines around his mouth, deep-scored. Carla stared at him, a stone in her chest. Then Cesare went on speaking, crossing his legs as if restless yet forced to sit still. Forced to endure what he was enduring.

'When we are in a position to formally announce our engagement,' he said, his voice coming from somewhere very distant, 'you will come to the *castello* and take up residence there. We shall be married in the chapel and—'

'No!' Once again Carla's defiant voice cut across him. Her chin went up and her eyes were burning violet. 'There will be only a civil ceremony. Nothing more. That way…' She took a ragged breath. 'That way we can divorce, without impediment to your future marriage.'

His brows snapped together. 'What are you saying?' he demanded.

'What has to be said! Oh, Cesare, if this is something we really have to do, then in God's name let us do it so that it does the least damage possible!'

She ran her fingertips over her brow. She was hot suddenly, despite the shade, hot and breathless. How could she sit here with Cesare in this dreadful mockery, this travesty?

Her voice dropped. 'Cesare, we can't do anything else. A civil marriage to legitimise the birth, and then a civilised divorce.'

He was looking at her. 'If you bear a son, he must be raised to his heritage,' he said.

She looked at him. 'Let me pray for a girl, then—that would solve everything, wouldn't it, Cesare? A girl who can grow up with me and leave you free to marry the woman you want to marry and have your heir with. Wouldn't that be the best? *Wouldn't* it?'

He was looking at her, a strange expression on his face. She could not read it—but not because it was shuttered. Because there was something in it she had never seen before.

'Is the thought of marriage to me so repulsive to you, Carla?'

She dropped her eyes. She had to. What could she say?

It would be unbearable! Unbearable to be married to you...loving you so much and yet being such a burden to you! Someone you don't want— who is forcing herself on you simply because she's carrying your child!

She swallowed. That jagged knife was in her throat now. She forced her eyes back to his, reaching for her coffee, making herself drink it.

'No more than it is repulsive for you to marry me,' she said, her voice low.

His gaze was on her—that strange, unreadable gaze that she could not recognise.

'I don't see why it should be repulsive at all,' he said slowly, his eyes never leaving her. He took a breath. 'After all, our time together showed we are, in fact, highly compatible. Neither of us were ever bored in each other's company.'

As he spoke memory flickered in his head. Not of Carla, but of the dinner party with Francesca, in the USA, with all her physics colleagues talking about things he had not the faintest comprehension of. With Carla it had been quite different—

At the choking point of their leash, he could feel his emotions straining to be free. Unleashed. One, at least, he *could* set free, granting him release.

His long lashes dipped over his eyes, clearing them, leaving them with an expression that Carla recognised only too well, that drew from her a tremor that was deep inside her.

'And sexually, of course, we are highly compatible.'

His gaze rested on her, only momentarily, but for long enough to send colour flaring out into her heated cheeks. She tore her gaze away, clattered her cup back on its saucer, stared out over the sparkling azure water of the pool, suddenly longing for its cooling depths.

The blood was beating in her veins, hot and hectic. Cesare was speaking again, and she heard his words, heard the sensual languor in them that only heated her blood the more.

'You must let me know, Carla, when it is safe for us to resume physical closeness. I know that in the early months it is not advised, but—'

She pushed back her chair, scraping it on the stone. 'I… I need to lie down!' Her voice was high-pitched, and even as she said the words she felt her colour mount.

He was on his feet too, his emotions back under control, back on their leash. 'Of course,' he said. 'You must rest.'

He glanced at his watch. Then back at Carla. Carla, the woman for whom, for all the complications and confusion and complexity, he felt one emotion that was very, very simple.

Desire.

He had desired her the moment he'd set eyes on her. He desired her still. That was undeniable—*that* was the emotion he knew he was safe with.

But not at this moment. Indulging it at this early stage of her pregnancy was out of the question, he knew, and for that one reason he must take himself off—let alone for all the other reasons assailing him.

'If you will permit, I will take my leave of you. I'm afraid I must return to the *castello*. I will be away, I fear, for several days. There is a great deal to be sorted out.'

Was there grimness in his voice? Carla looked at his shuttered expression. She was sure there was—and knew the reason. What else could it be for him but grim to perform the unwelcome task of telling his fiancée she'd been usurped by the extreme inconvenience of his former mistress becoming unexpectedly pregnant, requiring a swift marriage to satisfy the exacting terms of his sense of self-respect and familial honour?

She felt bleakness go through her. A sense of unreality. Yet this was real—all too real. That jagged blade drew across her heart again, sending a shot of agony through her. To have her heart's desire—marriage to Cesare—and yet for it to be like this was a travesty. An agony.

How can I do this? How? Cesare is forcing himself to marry me—just as I tried to force Vito to marry me. Is that all I'm good for? Forcing men to marry me?

A bead of hysteria bubbled in her throat. She swayed. Instantly Cesare was there, his hand strong under her elbow, steadying her. She felt his hand like a brand upon her.

'Are you all right?'

There was concern in his voice, and his eyes flickered to her abdomen, where only the slightest curve of her figure indicated her pregnancy. It was hardly visible yet—it had taken Vito's bear hug to reveal it to him, as he felt the swell below her waistline.

Vito, whom she had sought to use as a sticking plaster over her broken heart. Broken by the man her pregnancy was now forcing her to marry. Unbearable—just unbearable!

She turned her head to him, her eyes wild. 'Cesare, I can't make you marry me like this! I can't face another unwilling bridegroom! I forced Vito to the altar, using the threat of my mother selling his uncle's shares to Falcone, because I felt so…' She swallowed, finding a word that she could use to Cesare. 'So humiliated.'

She stepped away, taking a huge and painful breath, making herself look at him, her expression troubled, stricken.

'*So* humiliated, Cesare.' She watched his face close up, but went on all the same. 'I tried so hard while we were together—to be the woman you wanted me to be. I never pushed our relationship, never made demands on you.' She paused, remembering the dreadful, hideous moment when he had told her he was leaving. 'And I know you told me you'd never given me reason to expect anything more than what we had. But all the same, when you left me—'

She broke off, her throat thickening. Nearly—so nearly—she had blurted out what she must never, never tell him! What would be the ultimate humiliation for her. The ultimate burden on him.

He must never know I fell in love with him! Never!

He stepped towards her, then halted. There was something in his face again—that same look she had not understood before. Did not understand now.

'I was brutal to you that morning,' he said. There was reproof in his voice. Harshness. But not for her. 'Unforgivably so. But it was be-cause—'

He frowned, and she saw him making his next words come, making himself hold her gaze.

'It was because I did not want to part with you,' he said. He shifted restlessly, altering his stance. 'I didn't want to end our relationship. But my hand had been forced. Francesca needed a deci-sion—'

She saw his hand lift, as if he would reach for her, then drop again. She felt emotion welling in her, but did not know what, or how, or why.

'I had to give you up—and I was not pleased to have to do so. I knew I had to make the ending—swift. I never meant…' His eyes rested on hers. 'I never meant for you to feel what you said you felt.' His voice dropped. 'I never meant for you to feel humiliated by my rejection.'

He shook his head slowly, as if clearing it of things he had never thought about. His eyes fixed on hers again.

'I always respected you, Carla. Always. I still do. And if…' He took a heavy breath and she watched the breadth of his powerful chest widen with it. 'If I have seemed…distant, then think only that this has been a shock to me. Less than twenty-four hours ago…' his voice changed '…I saw my life, my future, quite differently from now.'

'I'm sorry,' she said, her voice low. 'So sorry for what has happened.'

'Don't be! It is not of your making. I take full responsibility! My behaviour that night—when I learnt you had not married Viscari—was unforgivable! No wonder you fled from me!' He paused for a moment, his face working. 'But if you had not fled before I woke, then perhaps—'

He stopped, as if silencing himself. His expression changed again. 'This is not the time for further talk,' he said.

He was finishing their discussion, she could see.

'We will have leisure for that ahead of us. For now—well, America is waking up, and I cannot in all conscience delay contacting Francesca.' He glanced at his watch, all businesslike now. 'So I will take my leave of you—for now. I will phone you this evening.'

She nodded wordlessly, and started to walk back indoors. Cesare fell into place beside her. Side by side—yet separate.

Her eyes went to the pair of elegant silk-upholstered sofas by the fireplace.

That's where he first started to make love to me. The night that he carried me upstairs, began our affair. Made me his.

But he was never hers. *Never.* Not even now, when he was forcing himself to marry her for the sake of the child she carried. The as yet unreal being who would become, as the months yielded to each other, so very, very real. Binding them to each other with an indissoluble bond, even if she were to divorce him and he was to marry—belatedly—his aristocratic Francesca.

This child will bind us to each other for ever. With him wishing it were not so and me...me haunted by what can never be. I can never be the woman he loves.

Into her head came the images on that triptych—the paintings that had catalysed their affair so many months ago. The Count flanked by the two women in his life. The peasant girl, gowned in red silk, who could never aspire to be his wife. And his pale, haunted wife, dutifully married, bonded for life, whether or not she had ever wanted to be.

I've become them both. The mistress he kept for his bed and the wife he married for duty, for a legitimate heir. Neither woman was happy. How could they be?

The bitterness was in her throat. Her heart.

They reached the cool, marbled hallway.

'Shall I see you up to your room?'

Cesare's voice penetrated her dark, bleak thoughts.

She shook her head. 'No—it's fine. I remember the way.'

She hadn't meant to sound sarcastic, and hoped she hadn't. Cesare did not seem to notice anyway. He only nodded.

He took her hands, holding them lightly but in a clasp she could not easily pull away from. His eyes looked into hers.

'Carla—I'm… I'm sorry. Sorry for so much. But however…however difficult things are to start with, you have my word that I will do my best—my very best—to be a good husband to you.'

His gaze held hers, but she found it hard…impossible…to bear it.

'I have said that we can make this work, and we can.' He took a breath. 'We can have a very civilised marriage. If we do divorce, at some later date—well, that is not for now. It is for then. And it may not come to that.'

For a moment it was as if he might say something more. She saw a tic in his cheek—indicating, she knew, that he was holding himself in strict self-control.

She drew back her hands. 'Cesare—go. There isn't anything more to say.' Her gaze slid away, not wanting to meet his. Heaviness weighed her down.

Be careful what you long for.

The warning sounded in her head. Once she had longed to become Cesare's wife—but not like this. Oh, not like *this*!

'Very well—I will take my leave, then.'

He did not make any gesture of farewell. Once, long ago, he would have dropped a swift, possessing kiss upon her lips, as if it were the seal of possession for their next time together. Now she was carrying his child, and that was seal of possession enough.

Except that I am a possession he does not want...

'Goodbye, Cesare.'

She did not say any more. What *could* she say? She'd said everything that could be said. Now they were simply bound to the motions they would need to go through.

She stepped back, waiting for him to leave. But suddenly, impulsively, he took her shoulders, dropped onto her forehead a brief flash of his lips. She felt his hands pressing on her shoulders, the shock of his mouth on her skin.

'We *can* make this work, Carla.'

There was intensity in his voice, in his eyes, pouring into hers. Then he was releasing her, striding away, throwing open the doors and moving out into the sunshine beyond to climb into his car and drive away.

Carla stood, listening to the engine fade into the distance. She walked forward to close the doors. Then slowly, very slowly, went upstairs.

How could they make it work? *How?*

Impossible...

CHAPTER ELEVEN

WITH SURE, SWIFT STEPS, Cesare headed down the winding pathway through the ornamental gardens below the elegant south-facing frontage of the *castello*, down into the deep valley where the narrow river rushed noisily over the boulders and rocks in its bed.

His stride was purposeful. He knew he should be contacting Francesca, but he could not face it—not yet. Instead he was doing what he had so often done as a boy, when he'd been seeking distance from the father he'd never been able to get on with.

By the river's edge he settled himself against an outcrop of rock in the late-afternoon sun, overlooking the tumbling water, fresh and cold and clean. Here, so often in his boyhood, he had found refuge from his father's admonitions and reproofs in watching the wading birds darting, in lying back on sun-warmed stone, hearing the wind soughing in the forest trees. Feeling the deep, eternal bond he had with this domain—the land that was in his blood, in his bones.

How many other Mondave sons had done likewise over the centuries? Waiting to step into their father's shoes, to take over the birthright to which they had been born?

And now, already, another son might be preparing to be born.

Out of nowhere the realisation hit him. Stilling every muscle in his body.

She carries my child! Perhaps my son—my heir!

The arc of the sky seemed to wheel about him and he took a shuddering breath. She was not the woman he had thought he would marry. In a single night, with a single act of tumultuous consummation, he had changed his own destiny. He felt emotion convulse in him. Carla—*Carla* would be his wife. Not Francesca. Carla carried his child. Carla would become his *contessa*.

He could feel the blood beating in his veins. Memory flashed through him—memory after memory. All the nights, all the days he'd spent with her. The sensual intensity of her body in his arms. The casual companionship of their times together.

I did not wish to part with her when I did.

He had told her that truthfully. Admitted it to her—to himself.

Yet into his head came her bitter words to him. 'You'd be marrying your mistress.'

His expression stilled, becoming masklike. Distant.

Is this what I want?

But what did it matter? His own desires were irrelevant. They always had been.

He had changed his own destiny. And now he had no choice but to marry Carla and set aside the woman whom he had always cast in the role of *contessa*. In his inner vision, the portraits in the triptych imposed themselves. The two women—the mistress and the wife—flanking his ancestor. The ancestor who had never had to change his own destiny.

He had them both—the mistress and the wife.

His eyes, as he gazed back towards at the *cas-*

tello, were suddenly grave. His destiny was to continue the ancient lineage of this house.

Always I've had to follow the path set out for me—first my duties to my inheritance, then my duty to marry Francesca, and now I am set by my honour to marry Carla, who carries my child. Choice has never been a possibility.

Slowly, his expression still grave, he got to his feet, made his way back to the *castello*, let himself into the drawing room. Walking through it, he moved out beyond into the state apartments, up the great staircase to the *galleria* above. Knowing just where he was going—and why.

The triptych at the far end was waiting for him. He walked up to it, looked into the face of his ancestor. *Proud*, Carla had called him, and he had taken her to task for it. She had not liked him, his ancestor, had seen only self-satisfaction, an overweening consciousness of his own sense of superiority as a man above others, taking whatever he wanted from life and paying no price for it.

Cesare's eyes went to the pale blonde woman to his ancestor's right. The woman he had married. *Chosen* to marry. Fingering her rosary, she had her prayer book on her lap, a poignant air and an expression of otherworldliness. As if she longed to be elsewhere. As if the sorrows of her life were too great to bear.

His eyes slid away to the other portrait—the other woman, his mistress. *Chosen* to be his mistress. The rich satin gown, the heavy jewels draped over her, the roses in her lap, a symbol of passion, and the ripe swell of her belly. The expression in her eyes showed her consciousness of her illicit relationship with his ancestor.

His ancestor had been free to choose them both. To pay no price for either.

Again Cesare's eyes slid away, back to the portrait of his ancestor. Saw the long-fingered hand, so like his own, closed over the pommel of his sword. His eyes went upwards to the face that Luciezo had preserved for all posterity. For *him*, his descendant, to look upon and contemplate.

For the first time, as he stood there, so sombrely regarding his ancestor's face, he saw something in those dark, brooding eyes—a shadow around the sculpted mouth…a tightness. A tension. As if his gilded, privileged life had not been entirely to his pleasure. Not entirely what he'd wanted...

Across the centuries that divided them Cesare's eyes held those of his ancestor. As if he would divine his innermost thoughts. Drill across the centuries to see inside the man whose blood ran in his veins.

A tightness shaped itself around his own mouth—a tension.

Abruptly, he turned away. Walking with rapid strides, he moved back down the lofty length of the *galleria*, descending the stairs with clattering heels. He walked into the library with its vast array of shelves, its acres of tomes inset.

His archivist was there, working on some research project or other requested by some university's history department. He started as Cesare walked in, and got to his feet.

'Tell me, are there any personal diaries or journals from Count Alessandro—the one Luciezo painted for the triptych?' Cesare asked without preamble.

His archivist blinked. 'I would need to check...' he answered uncertainly.

'Do so, if you please. And anything that you find, have sent to my office. Thank you.'

Cesare took his leave briskly, wondering to himself what impulse had made him make such a request—wondering what he had glimpsed in his ancestor's impassive face.

He pulled his mind away. He had no time to brood further. He must phone Francesca. That could not be postponed any longer.

His brows drew together. Was this really something that could be said over the phone? Telling her that he could no longer marry her? His frown deepened. He owed her more than that, surely— more than a cursory phone call.

I have to tell her to her face—I owe her that courtesy, that consideration, at least.

He would be changing her expected destiny, just as his was now changed.

He gave a heavy sigh, sitting himself down at the desk in his office, calling up airline websites, seeing when he could fly out.

He would have to tell Carla what he was doing. She would understand. He would be away a handful of days—no more than that, allowing for time differences across the Atlantic. Then he would return and announce his engagement to Carla.

Carla lay in bed, listening to the dawn chorus. She had scarcely slept. She had spent the remainder of the previous day, after Cesare had left, lying on her bed, sleepless, and then restlessly going down to the pool, immersing herself in the cooling water.

As she'd worked her way up and down in a slow breaststroke she'd felt a kind of numbness steal over her. It had lasted through the evening, through dinner—served with Lorenzo's usual skilful unobtrusiveness—and even through the phone call that Cesare had dutifully made.

Conversation had been awkward—how could it have been otherwise?—and after enquiring how she was, and how she had spent the rest of the day, his voice constrained, he had informed her in an even more constrained fashion that he would be flying to the USA the next day to see Francesca.

She had been understanding of his reasons—

but as she'd hung up she'd felt a wave of guilt go through her.

He didn't ask for this! He didn't ask for me to present him with my pregnancy, turning his life upside down as it has!

And the woman who'd thought she would be marrying Cesare—*her* life was being turned upside down as well. Ripped out from under her.

By me—by my giving in and agreeing to marry Cesare. Who feels he has no choice but to marry me.

Just as she had tried to force Vito to marry her. Making him do what she wanted. Ripping up his life. Ripping up the life he had been planning to make with that blonde English girl he was now so urgently seeking.

She closed her eyes in misery.

Haven't I done enough damage to people? Do I have to ruin Cesare's life too—and his fiancée's?

The knowledge hung darkly, bleakly inside her.

Silently, she ran her mind back, thinking of the father she could not remember—had scarcely known. For the first time she thought of how he must have felt, told that he had to marry a woman he did not love because she carried his child. Had he had other plans? Other dreams? Dreams that had been smashed to pieces? Of a life he'd wanted to live and that had been barred to him?

Just as her pregnancy was barring Cesare from having the life *he* wanted. Requiring him to do his duty, take *her* for his wife instead of the woman he wanted to marry.

A cry sounded in her head.

I don't want to force Cesare to marry me!

She felt her heart constrict. Memory poured in around it.

I had my happiness here—as much as I could ever have with Cesare. I knew from the start it was all I could have with him. That he could never be mine—not the way I came to long for him to be.

She felt her eyes distend, looking back into the past, the days and nights she had spent with Cesare. Then looking into the future she had now committed herself to—becoming his wife, his *contessa*, but not the one he had chosen of his own free will.

I can't do this to him.

With a sudden impulse she threw back the bed-clothes, her hand automatically easing across her abdomen as she got up. Inside—invisible, almost intangible—new life was growing.

She felt her throat close with sudden, overpowering emotion.

This is Cesare's gift to me. Not his heart, but his child. And it will be enough.

With swift, resolute movements she dressed, re-packed her case, headed downstairs. She needed to find Lorenzo—needed him to summon her a taxi to the airport. Needed to do what she knew she must do—set Cesare free.

With heavy tread Cesare walked down the ornate staircase to the *piano nobile* of the eighteenth-century section of the *castello*. He was booked on a flight to the USA, and his helicopter pilot was on standby now to fly him to the airport. He'd emailed Francesca last night, to let her know of his impending visit—but had given no indication of his purpose. It would be a shock to her, what he must tell her, but it was one he had no choice but to inflict.

Yet again, as it had done the previous afternoon, across his mind flashed the image of that Luciezo portrait. The ancestor who had had complete freedom of choice in his life. He ejected the image. What was the point of thinking about his forebear? His own life afforded no such freedom of choice.

Abruptly he went into his office, snapped on his laptop, dragging his mind back to the present and all the difficulties that enmeshed him. He must check to see if Francesca had replied to his email. She had—but it took him a moment to steel himself to open it. The enormity of what he was going to have to do to her weighed upon him. She did not deserve it.

Yet nor does Carla deserve to have to marry me. She made it clear enough to me yesterday how reluctant she is!

And he—what did *he* feel about it?

He veered his mind away. That was a path he did not wish to follow. Not now. Not yet. First he must smash up Francesca's life.

He clicked open her email. Made himself focus

on what she had written. For an instant, her words blurred, then resolved.

He started to read.

My dearest Ces, your email has been a catalyst for me. I have something I can no longer delay telling you.

He read on, disbelievingly.

Then, as the full impact of what she had written hit him, he sat back, his chest tight. Slowly he reached to close down his laptop. He would reply—but not yet. For now he could only sit there. Taking in what she had written. Taking in the implications.

A discreet knock sounded on his office door. At his abstracted permission to enter, his archivist came in.

'The papers you asked after yesterday,' he said, placing a leather-bound folder in front of Cesare. 'This is Count Alessandro's private journal.'

Cesare thanked him, his manner still absent, his mind still elsewhere. Then, as if to shake his thoughts from him, he reached for the folder and opened it, bringing out a marbled notebook, its pages mottled with age, covered in thin, flowing script. Sixteenth-century Italian, difficult to decipher.

But across the centuries his ancestor's words reached to him. And as he read a frown started across his face. He read on in silence, his expression sombre. Then, at last, he lifted his eyes from the page, from the ink scored so deeply into the antique paper, as if reverberating still with the vehemence of his ancestor.

For a long while he sat. Feeling emotion swirl deep within him—turbid, inchoate. Making sense of what he'd read. Seeing, too, the printed words on his screen—Francesca's email—melding with the antique script in front of him.

Then, with a sudden intake of breath, he pushed back his chair. He needed to stand down his helicopter pilot. And he needed to drive back to Lazio.

He was halfway to the door when he felt his phone vibrate in his jacket pocket. He pulled it out, glanced at the screen.

A voicemail.

From Carla.

He stilled. Pressed 'play'.

And everything in his world changed again...

CHAPTER TWELVE

CARLA WAS SWIMMING—slowly but steadily ploughing up and down the length of the pool at her mother's villa. Had it really only been a week since she'd made her decision to set Cesare free?

As she climbed out of the water she felt a familiar tightening of her chest—an ache of emotion burning within her. Regret? Could it be that? Regret at having walked away from the one chance she would have to be part of Cesare's life?

No—marriage to Cesare like that would have been unbearable! She had told him so, and it was true. True, true, *true*. So that was what she must hold to—all that must guide her now. However hard it was.

'Darling, are you all right? You mustn't overdo it.'

Marlene's voice was concerned as she hurried

forward with an enveloping towel, draping it around Carla's wet back.

Carla smiled her thanks, taking a seat in the sunshine while her mother fussed about her. Her mother had been fussing…hovering…ever since she'd arrived back from Italy. And as she'd heard her daughter out Carla had seen the reaction in her face.

'He's offered to *marry* you?' she'd said.

Her eyes had worked over Carla. Then slid away into her own past.

'The decision must be yours,' Marlene had said slowly. 'But for my part I think it's the right one—the decision you've made.' She'd paused a moment before continuing. 'Marrying your father was the worst mistake I made. I'd hoped it would make him love me. But it did the opposite. He married me because of pressure from his father, who held the purse strings and did not want any scandal. But when his father died— you were only a toddler—he took off.' She'd paused again. 'When he was killed in that car crash there was a woman with him—and he'd just filed for divorce.'

She'd looked at her daughter, her eyes troubled.

'I ruined his life—and marriage brought no happiness for me either.' She'd taken a breath, exhaled sadly. 'No happy ending—for me *or* for him.'

No happy ending...

The words hovered in Carla's mind. Her mother's sorry tale only confirmed the rightness of her decision to leave Italy, to tell Cesare in that solitary voicemail that it was all she could face doing—that she preferred single motherhood to forcing him to marry her instead of the woman he wanted to marry.

'Go back to her, Cesare, and make the marriage you have always been destined to make. I don't want to be the one to part you from her— not for any reason. She is the woman you chose for your wife, not me. The time we had together was very...very special to me. But it is over. I wish you well. This is my choice. Please do not try and dissuade me from it.'

She had had no reply. Knew that she must be glad she had not. Knew that she must be glad she had set him free. Must bear the pain that came with that.

To have nothing of him... Nothing—just as I had when he left me—nothing of him.

Yet as she sat sipping at her iced fruit juice, feeling the Spanish summer heat warm her damp limbs, her hand slipped to curve around the swell of her abdomen.

No, not nothing. This is Cesare's gift to me.

And memories—memories that she would never lose. *Never!*

Cesare reaching for her, taking her mouth with his, slow and seductive, arousing and sensual, taking his fill of her as her hands stroked his smooth, hard body, glorying in the feel of it beneath her exploring, delicately circling fingertips.

Cesare, his body melded with hers in the white heat of passion, desire burning with a searing flame, until she cried out, her body arching in ecstasy, the ecstasy of his possession...

A possession she could never know again.

She felt that ache form in her chest again, around her heart. An ache that would never leave her. Could never leave her. The ache of a broken heart that could never mend. She could never have the man she loved, loving her in return.

No happy ending…

Cesare walked up the wide, imposing staircase to the panelled, gilded *galleria*. Along the walls priceless Old Masters marched on either side. But he did not look at them. He went only to the far end of the long room. Stood before the triptych, letting his eyes rest on the three portraits, thinking of their tangled, entwined lives.

Once he had thought he knew them…presumed to know them…these three people from so long ago. Thought to know his ancestor, whose blood ran in his veins. The ancestor who had been free to choose, flanked by the women either side of him. The woman he'd chosen for his wife. The woman he'd chosen for his mistress.

Free to choose.

Abruptly, he turned away. Nodded at the two men waiting patiently at the entrance to the *galleria*.

'You can remove it now,' he told them.

Without a backward glance, he walked out of the room.

His expression was unreadable. But emotion was heavy within him. Weighing him down. In his head he heard, over and over again, as he had done since he had first listened to her voicemail, Carla's farewell to him.

'This is my choice. Please do not try and dissuade me from it.'

Behind him he heard the sounds of the triptych being taken down, dismantled. Packed up.

He walked on, face set.

Carla was breakfasting with her mother. The weather was cooler today now, and she was glad. Glad, too, that by the time she was in late pregnancy she would be cooler still.

As it did so often, her hand glided protectively over her abdomen. Her thoughts were full. She must stay calm, serene. Let no agitation break through—no emotion or trauma. She had chosen this path—single motherhood—over a tormented marriage to Cesare. It had been the right choice to make.

Her expression changed. Vito was appalled that she was not going to marry Cesare, but she remained adamant. She would not be swayed. And, for himself, Vito had finally found a ray of hope in his search for the woman she had caused to flee. She might have been located at last. She wished him well—hoped that he would find the happiness he sought.

As for herself—well, happiness was beyond her now. Cesare had accepted her decision. She had heard nothing more from him.

I grew up fatherless, and my child will too. But it will have me, and my mother, and safety and love, and that is all that really matters.

That was what she told herself. That was what she must believe. As for Cesare—well, he would marry his *marchese*'s daughter and live the life he had always planned.

And I will have his child—his gift to me.

It was more than she had ever hoped to have of him. She must be content with that. In time her battered heart would heal, and Cesare would have no place in it any longer.

A sliver of pain pierced her, but she ignored

it. Soon, surely, it would cease. The ache in her heart would ease. It must.

It *must*.

'The mail, *señora*.'

Her mother's maid was placing a stash of post on the table, breaking Carla's painful reverie. Idly, she watched her mother sort it, then pause.

'This is for you,' she said, holding up a bulky envelope, her expression wary.

Carla felt herself tense—the stamp was Italian, the dark, decisive handwriting instantly recognisable. Steeling herself, she opened it, taking out several folded papers.

It will be some sort of legal document I have to sign, foregoing any claim on his estate for the baby, or a contract making me a maintenance allowance or something.

But as she unfolded them she gasped. It was neither of those things.

'Darling, what is it?' Marlene's voice was immediately alarmed.

Carla stared, then looked blankly across at her mother. In a hollow voice she spoke. 'It's from a secure art vault in Rome. It tells me…' She swallowed. 'It tells me that the Luciezo-Caradino triptych is now in storage. That it is being held in trust—for...for...'

Instinctively her hand went to her ripening abdomen, her eyes distending. She dropped the letter, seized up the piece of paper with Cesare's handwriting, and the third folded document.

'Mum, I—I—'

She could say no more—only got to her feet, stumbling slightly as she walked away, past the pool, to find the bench underneath the shade of the bougainvillea arbour, overlooking the beach.

She sat down with trembling legs. Opened Cesare's letter to read it. The writing came into focus, burned into her retinas—Cesare's words to her.

I have made this bequest to you not only for the child you carry but as a token—a symbol of what is between us. To understand why, I ask you to read the enclosed. It is a typed transcript from the personal diary of Count Alessandro, who was portrayed by Luciezo.

Read it now, before you read more of this letter.

She let the page fall to her lap, then unfolded the transcript with fumbling fingers. Made herself read it. The Italian was old-fashioned, with some words she did not know. But as she read she felt the world shift and rearrange itself.

Slowly, with a hollow feeling within her, she set it aside, picked up Cesare's letter again. Resumed reading.

It was brief.

I will not make the mistake he made. Whatever decision you now make, know that I am not my ancestor.

It was signed starkly, simply, with his name: *Cesare.*

Carefully—very, very carefully—her heart hammering in her chest, she put the papers back in the envelope. Then she went up onto the patio, where her mother was anxiously looking for her.

Marlene started to get to her feet, but Carla stayed her.

'I have to go to him,' she said.

Her voice was strange. Hollow. Her heart was filling with an emotion she could feel overwhelming her, drowning her.

The hire car ate up the miles, racing along the *autostrada* across the lush countryside of Lazio as she snaked ever upwards into the mountainous terrain, gaining at last, as darkness fell, the mighty stone entrance to the massive bulk of the Castello Mantegna.

I will not make the mistake he made.

Slowly, she made her way to the gate, looked at the walls of the *castello* louring over her. A postern door was set into the towering iron-studded gates, with an ancient metal bell-pull beside it. And a more modern intercom and surveillance camera.

She pressed the buzzer, giving her name. There was silence—complete and absolute silence. No response at all from within that stony fastness.

Her head sank. Defeat was in the slump of her shoulders.

Fool! Oh—fool, fool, fool!

The words berated her, like blows.

'Signorina! Prego—prego!'

The man at the now open postern gate was in the uniform of a security guard—which, Carla realised dimly, given the value of the artworks within, even without the priceless triptych, made sense. He was beckoning her frantically.

Heart in her mouth, she stepped inside, through the gate into the vast, cobbled courtyard within. The guard was apologising fervently, but her eyes were darting either side to the ranks of former stables, now garaging, and the old medieval kitchens, now staff and estate office quarters. Both wings were utterly dominated by the huge mass of the *castello* itself, rising darkly ahead of her.

Dusk was gathering in this huge paved courtyard, and security lights were coming on as she was conducted across it to a pair of palatial iron-studded doors that were being thrown open even as she spoke. Inside, she could see a huge, cavernous hall, brilliantly lit with massive candelabras. And across it, striding rapidly, came the figure of the man she had come to brave in his mountain fastness.

Cesare di Mondave, Conte di Mantegna, lord of his domain…

Faintness drummed at her. The effects of her early start that morning—after a night in which the hours had passed sleepless and tormented with confusion, with emotions that had pummelled through her mercilessly, relentlessly— the drive to the airport, the flight to Rome, the disembarking, the hiring of the car, the journey here. Exhaustion weighed her down like a heavy, smothering coat. Her nerves were shattered, her strength gone.

She sank downwards.

He was there instantly, with an oath, catching her. Catching her up into his arms, even though she weighed more now than she had ever done, as her body ripened with its precious burden. But as if she were a feather he bore her off. She closed her eyes, head sinking onto his shoulder. Feeling his strength, his warmth, his very scent…

Cesare.

His name soared in her head, fighting through

the clouds, the thick mist that surrounded her. He was going through doorways, up a marble staircase, all the while casting urgent, abrupt instructions at those whose footsteps she heard running. There were anxious voices, male and female, until at the last she was lowered down upon the softest counterpane. She sank into it and her eyes fluttered. She was lying on a vast, ornate four-poster, silk-hung, and lights were springing up everywhere. Cesare was hovering above her, and there was a bevy of people, so it seemed, behind him.

'*Il dottore!* Get him here—now!'

There was command—stern, urgent—in that deep voice. Obedience in the one that answered it.

'*Si! Si!* At once—at once. He is summoned!'

She struggled upright, emotion surging through her again, past the tide of faintness. 'No…no… I don't need a doctor—I'm fine… I'm fine.'

Cesare looked down at her. The room, she realised, was suddenly empty. There was only him, towering over her.

'He is on his way, nevertheless,' he said.

There was still command in his voice. Then his expression changed. His gaze speared into hers, and in his face Carla saw something that stopped the breath in her body.

'Why did you come? Tell me—*Dio mio*—*tell me!*'

She had never heard him speak like that—with so much raw, vehement emotion in his voice. She felt an answering emotion in herself, yet dared not feel it...*dared* not.

Her eyes, so deep a violet, searched his, still not daring to believe.

Slowly, falteringly, she spoke. 'When you wrote...*what* you wrote—I read... I read Count Alessandro's words...and then yours...'

Her voice was strained, her words disjointed. Her eyes searched his. She still did not dare to believe. This was the man prepared to marry her out of duty, out of responsibility. So how could he have written what he had? *Why?* Once before she had allowed herself to hope—hope that his feelings might be starting to echo hers...the very night he'd told her he was leaving her. Destroying her—

So how could she dare to hope again? *Could* she dare? She had to *know*.

'Cesare, why…why did you write what you did? That you would not make the mistake he did?' Her voice was faint, low. Yet her eyes were wide, distended.

That same vehemence was in his face—the same emotion that was stopping the breath in her body, that she had never seen before in it. It had not been there—not once—in all the time she'd known him.

His eyes burned into hers. 'You read his words,' he said. 'He married his *contessa* from duty, from expectation. Yet she never wanted to marry him. Never wanted to marry at all. Her vocation was to become a nun. But her family forced her to marry, to do her duty, to bear his children as a noblewoman should do. And he—Count Alessandro—he did as a nobleman should do: protective of his honour, taking pride in his ancient name. He did not love her, his *contessa*—that was not relevant.'

In Carla's head she heard again what Cesare had said when he had informed her he was intending to marry—that loving Francesca, his intended wife, was not 'relevant'. As she remembered, as she gazed at him now, still not daring to believe, she felt the same emotion that had brought her here, to his ancient *castello*, driven by an urgency that had possessed her utterly.

'And yet...' She heard the fracture in Cesare's voice. 'And yet there was a woman he *did* love.' He paused, his eyes still spearing hers. 'It was his mistress. The mistress he had taken from desire, whom he had never thought to marry. It was his mistress with whom he spent his hours of leisure. And it was the family he had with *her*—for babies were impossible to stop in those times, as you know—that he loved. Not the solitary son he had with his *contessa*—the son who grew to manhood hating the father who so clearly had no time for him, no love. Just as he had no time, no love, for the son's mother, the Contessa.'

Abruptly he let go her hand, got to his feet. Thrusting his hands into his pockets, he strode to the windows overlooking the valley beyond. He spoke with his back to her, gazing out at the night beyond the panes of glass, as if he could see into it, through it, back into a past that was not the youth of Count Alessandro's heir—but his own youth.

'My father had no time for me,' he said.

His voice had changed. Thinned. He was speaking of things he never spoke of. But now he must.

'He thought me oversensitive! Unlike him, I did not think that being a brilliant shot, a hunter of game, of wildlife slaughtered to hang as trophies on his walls, was a worthy accomplishment, fitting for my rank. He despised me for what he called my squeamishness. Judged me for it. Condemned me. Openly told me I was not up to being his heir.'

He was silent a moment, and his lips pressed together. Then he went on.

'When he died I determined to prove myself—to prove him wrong. Oh, I still never took to his murderous love of slaughtering wildlife, but I immersed myself in the management of all the heritage that had come to me—the enterprises, the people in my employ, the tenants and clients, all those whom the estates support and who support the estates. I did my duty and beyond to all that my name and title demanded and required of me. I gave his ghost, the ghosts of *all* my ancestors, no cause at all to think me lacking!'

He turned now, looking back across the room to the figure lying propped up against the pillows on his bed, to the swell of her body visible now in the lamplight limning her features. He felt emotion move within him as he spoke on.

'And the final duty for me to discharge,' he said, his voice grave now, and his expression just as grave, 'was to marry. The final duty of all who bear my name and title is to marry and create a successor.'

His eyes shifted slightly, then came back to Carla. Her eyes were fixed on him, her face gaunt now.

Cesare took a breath. 'My father always approved of Francesca—always identified her as the ideal woman I should marry. She was suitable in every way—and he told me I would be fortunate indeed if she would agree to the match.'

He shut his eyes again, his face convulsing, then opened his eyes once more. Let his gaze rest unflinchingly on Carla.

'And so she would have been.' He stopped, his jaw tightening. 'If I had not met you.'

There was silence—complete silence.

'But when Francesca wrote to me, told me she had gained her doctorate earlier than she'd expected, she said she would need to choose between staying on in the USA and coming home to marry me.' He paused, his eyes looking inward, his mouth tightening. 'My first reaction to her letter should have told me.' His face twisted. 'Told me that I had changed profoundly. For my first reaction was immediate.' He paused. 'It was to cry out in my head, *Not yet!*'

His gaze came back to Carla.

'Instead—' He took a heavy breath. 'Instead I told myself how *ideal* marriage to Francesca would be. How entirely suited she was to be my wife…how well she would take on the role of my *contessa*. She knew all that it would entail and, unlike my own mother, who made being her husband's wife the sole reason for her existence, Francesca would continue her academic research here in Italy. When she gave me her decision I knew there was only one thing for me to do.' He paused again, and when he spoke his voice was heavier still. 'Remove you from my life'.

She had shut her eyes. He could see it—see how her fingers on the counterpane had spasmed suddenly.

His voice was quiet now, and yet she could hear every word as clearly, as distinctly as the space between them would allow.

'But there was a place I could not remove you from. A place I did not even know you had come to occupy.'

She could hear him now, in the darkness of her blinded vision.

'A place, Carla, where you will always be. That you can never be removed from. *Never!*'

The sudden vehemence in his voice made her eyes flare open. She could see his gaze burning at her.

'I did not know you were there, Carla! I did not know it even when I was filled with jealous rage—a rage I knew with my head that I had no right at all to feel. Yet it tore me apart all the same! When I heard that you'd become engaged to Vito Viscari—' His voice twisted.

'Madness overcame me that night I came to your apartment, blackly rejoicing that he had not married you.' His expression changed again, became gaunt and bleak. 'Even when Viscari told me that you carried my child—even then, Carla, when I knew we would marry, *must* marry, even then I did not realise.'

He stood still, hands thrust deep into his pockets, looking at her across the space that was between them.

'All I could think was how I'd never been permitted to choose—how first it had been my *duty* to marry Francesca, if she would have me, and then…' he took a ragged breath '…it became my *duty* to marry you instead.'

She shut her eyes for a moment, feeling the bleakness she had felt at knowing she was forcing Cesare to marry her. But he was speaking still, his voice changing yet again.

'When I came back here I found myself seeking out that Luciezo portrait—thinking how my ancestor had been free to choose whatever he willed, as I had never been. And yet—'

He broke off, his face working. Carla's eyes

were on him again, wide, distended, and her throat was tightening.

'Yet when I read his journal…' He exhaled slowly, his eyes never leaving hers, filled with a darkness that chilled her suddenly. 'When I read his final words, then—'

When he resumed, his voice was raw.

'He cursed himself—cursed what he had done, the choice that he had made in marrying a woman he could not love. He had blighted his whole life—and the lives of both his wife and his mistress, condemning them all to unhappiness. It was a mistake that could never be mended—*never*!'

Carla felt her own face work, her throat close.

Words burst from her, pained and anguished. 'That is what I felt *I* would do if I married you! It would be as if I had become *both* those Caradino portraits—the pregnant mistress becoming the unhappy wife!'

Her fingers clenched again, spasming.

'I knew you didn't want to marry me! How could you, when you'd chosen another woman to marry, had set me aside as you had? How could

I condemn you to a loveless marriage to me—condemn you to a marriage you'd never wanted?'

Her voice dropped.

'How could I condemn *myself* to it? Condemn myself to the kind of marriage my own mother made—and bitterly regretted. Just as my father regretted it. And…' Her throat closed painfully. 'Just as you would regret it too. Regret a loveless marriage—'

She broke off, emotion choking her voice. Her eyes closed, and it was as if she could feel sharp shards of glass beneath her lids. There was a sudden dip in the bed—the heavy weight of Cesare jackknifing down beside her. His hand closed over hers, stilling its clenching.

Her eyes flared open, diamond tears within.

Emotion was in his face, strong and powerful, sending a sudden surge to her pulse, a tightening of her throat. There was a searing in her heart against what he might say next.

'It would not be loveless.' Intensity infused his voice. 'It would *not* be loveless,' Cesare said again. 'When I read Alessandro's cry of despair and remorse for the mistake he had made, the mistake that could never be amended, I knew—finally *knew*—what I had blinded myself to! I realised, with a flash of lightning in my eyes, that I could leave you, or you could leave me, and it would make no difference—none at all. For you were lodged in that place from which you could never be removed.'

He paused. Eyes resting on her. The truth was in them, as he knew it must be now.

'In my heart, Carla. Where you will always be. *You* are the woman I would choose for my wife. Whether you carry our child or not.' He took a breath. 'I would choose *you*—because I love you.'

She heard his words—heard that one most precious word that was more to her than all the world—heard it and felt her heart fill with an emotion she could scarcely bear. Did she see the same emotion in his eyes?

She felt Cesare's strong hand press down on hers. Another ragged breath broke from him.

'*That* is what I wanted you to know. *Needed* you to know. You may not love me, Carla, but I *needed* you to know my heart. So that whatever choice you make now—whether to marry me or not—you know that you are in my heart for all time. And that you always will be.'

He took a shuddering breath. Poured all that he was into his next words.

'The choice is yours—it always will be—but if you feel…if you *can* feel even a fraction of what I feel for you, will you accept my hand, my heart, my life, my love?'

Carla felt her hand move beneath his. Curl into his. Hold his fast. Those diamond tears were still glittering in her eyes and she could not speak. She started to lift her free hand and in an instant he had caught it. Raised it slowly to his lips.

She saw his expression change, grow sombre again.

'Alessandro is dust,' he said. 'As are his wife and the woman he loved. For them all, his regret, his remorse, came too late. But we—' And yet again he broke off as strong emotion worked in his face. 'We live *now*—and we can make our future what we will. We can seize it, Carla—seize it and make it our own!'

His hands pressed hers.

'My most beloved *preciosa*, will you accept

my hand in marriage? Will you stand at my side all my life, as my beloved wife—my *contessa*? Will you give me the priceless gift of your heart, your love? Will you let the precious child within you be the proof and symbol of our love, our life together? Will you be...' his voice caught '...in one person, both my wife and the woman I love?'

His voice changed, became overwrought with emotion.

'Will you unite the triptych—not, as you feared, as an unhappy mistress becoming the unhappy wife, but in the way it *should* have been united? So that there is no division between wife and love—united in the same woman. United in *you*.'

She felt her heart turn over and fill to the brim with a joy she had never thought to feel.

Cesare, oh, Cesare—my Cesare!

He leant forward to kiss her tears away, then kissed her mouth. Her fingers clutched his as he drew away again.

'I tried not to fall in love with you,' she said, her voice low and strained. 'Right from the first, when we began our affair, I knew that that was all it could ever be. I knew all along there could be no future for us. That one day you would set me aside to make the kind of marriage I knew you must make. But I could not stop myself. I fell in love with you despite my warnings to myself. And when you ended it… I went into a kind of madness.'

Her face shadowed.

'I behaved despicably to Vito. I nearly ruined his life. That's why—' She took a ragged breath. 'That's why I realised I could not ruin your life when you did not love me. When you wanted to marry Francesca—'

She broke off, her expression changing suddenly.

'*Francesca!* Cesare—?' Concern was open in her voice.

He smiled. A wry, self-mocking smile. 'Francesca,' he said, 'has gone to California! It seems,' he went on, half rueful, half relieved, 'that she, too, did not wish to make a loveless marriage—or any marriage at all! She wrote to tell me that out of the blue she has been invited to join an ultra-prestigious research team on the West Coast, led by a Nobel laureate, and it is her heart's desire to take up the post. She is beside herself with excitement, and knows I will understand why she cannot marry me now after all.'

He smiled again, and Carla could see relief in it, as well as a self-deprecating ruefulness.

'Astrophysics is her love—not being my *contessa*!'

Carla's expression changed. 'Count Alessandro's wife wanted to be a nun…' she mused. 'That was *her* true calling.'

Cesare nodded, seeing the analogy. 'And scientific research is calling Francesca. For which—' he dropped a kiss on Carla's forehead '—I am profoundly grateful.' He smiled again. 'You will like her, you know, if she makes it to our wedding. But you will have to accept that you won't understand much of what fascinates her so.'

The wry look was back in his face again, and then his expression altered a little, and he frowned slightly.

'Maybe that was a warning to me—the fact that I found it hard to communicate with her about her work. Although I know she would always have discharged her responsibilities as Contessa, her heart would not have been in it. I think,' he said, 'it took our betrothal to make her realise that what she had grown up with—the expectation she'd always had of what her future was to be— was not, after all, what she wanted.' His voice grew sombre again now. 'Just as did I.'

He paused, his eyes holding Carla's. Then went on.

'I do not ask forgiveness for what I did to you— only for...understanding. If you can bring yourself to give me that, then—'

She did not let him finish. 'I give you both, Cesare—I understand *and* I forgive! From my heart—believe me!'

Her voice was broken with the urgency of what she said.

His expression changed again, lightening now, and he slid the palm of one hand across her abdomen, catching his breath as he felt the ripening curve of her body. For a moment he closed his eyes, almost unable to believe that this moment had come. A great peace had come upon him, filling his every cell, suffusing his body— his mind and his soul.

He leant towards her, his lips brushing hers, and Carla met them, her eyes fluttering shut as if to contain the immensity of the joy within her. His kiss was warm and deep, and in it were the seeds for a harvest of happiness she would reap all her life.

'My dearest heart,' Cesare said. 'My dearest love.'

He kissed her again—tenderly, cherishingly—this woman he loved, whom he had so nearly lost. Who would now be at his side and in his heart all his life.

For a long, long moment they simply held each other, feeling the closeness of their hearts, feeling the peace of love envelop them. Unite them.

'*My* Cesare,' she whispered.

For now he *was* hers—truly hers—and all her hopes had been fulfilled, all her fears and losses had gone for ever.

Her fingers slid around the strong nape of his neck, splaying into his raven hair. She knew he was hers and she was his. For all time—now and far beyond mere time.

There was the sound of a knock upon the door,

the door opening. Cesare's steward announced the doctor.

Cesare glanced at Carla. She had a look of dazed happiness on her face that made a smile curve at Cesare's mouth. Maybe the doctor was not needed. But the woman he loved carried a gift for them both that was infinitely precious.

After greeting the doctor, he left him to his examination and, out in the hall, gave instructions for the best vintage champagne in his extensive cellars to be fetched. Then, in time-honoured fashion he paced outside the bedroom door, until the doctor emerged.

'Well?' He pounced immediately.

The doctor nodded. 'Quite well,' he pronounced. 'Fatigue and an excess of emotion, that is all.' He cleared his throat. 'Would I be presumptuous,' he asked, his eyes slightly wary, 'in offering you, Signor Conte, my felicitations?'

Relief flooded through Cesare. He met the doctor's eyes. 'You would not,' he said decisively.

He spoke deliberately. His steward had returned, ready to show the doctor out. The words Cesare had spoken would be all his steward would require. Within ten minutes every person in the *castello* would know that a different chatelaine from the one they had been expecting would now be in their future.

His heart, as he went back into his bedroom, was soaring. Carla possessed the one attribute that was all he needed in his wife.

She is the woman I love—and will love all my days.

And he was the man she loved.

What else could matter but that? *That* was what his ancestor Alessandro had taught him, through his own heart-wrenching regret.

I will not make the mistake he made.

The words seared in his consciousness again as he swept Carla—the woman he loved—into his arms.

'The doctor tells me all is well.'

His eyes were warm—so warm—and Carla felt her heart turn over. Could she really be this happy? Could she truly be this happy? And yet she was.

This is real, and it is true—it is not my mere hopes and dreams!

Wonder filled her, and then pierced even more as Cesare drew back and with a sudden movement did what she had never seen him do before. He took from his little finger the signet ring engraved with the crest of his house, which he *never* removed—not for bathing, or swimming, or for any reason—and then reached for her hand again.

His eyes went to her. 'For my *contessa*,' he said, and slid the ring, still warm from his skin, onto her finger.

Then he closed his hand over hers, knuckling her hand under his. He smiled.

'There's actually a signet ring specifically for the Contessa,' he said. 'My mother wore it always from her wedding day. But for tonight, my dearest love, as we celebrate this moment, wear my ring, which I have never taken from my finger since the day I placed it there—the day my father died.'

She felt her throat catch. So simple a gesture—so profound a meaning. She felt tears well in her eyes again. His hand tightened over hers.

'No more tears!' he commanded. 'I will not permit it!'

Her face quivered into tearful laughter. 'There speaks *il Conte*!'

'Indeed he does,' he agreed, patting her hand.

He dropped a kiss on her forehead, then started to draw her to her feet.

'If you feel ready, *mi amore*, can you face my household? My steward will now have informed everyone of our news, and I have ordered champagne to be served in the salon. One glass, I am sure, will not harm our child.'

He helped her stand up, and walked with her to the door.

'And then I am sure you will wish to phone your mother, will you not? I hope she will be glad for you now that she need have no fear that you are repeating her own experience of marriage, and now that she knows how much I love you.'

His expression softened, and Carla felt again that wash of bliss go through her.

Then another emotion caught her. She halted.

'Cesare—my mother is…controversial,' she said uneasily. 'When she sold Guido Viscari's shares after Vito refused to marry me, Lucia ensured she became *persona non grata* in Rome—'

'I think you will find,' replied Cesare, his voice dry and edged with hauteur, 'that as my mother-in-law, and grandmother to my heir, she will find *no* doors closed to her—in Rome, or anywhere else!'

Carla smiled. 'Thank you,' she acknowledged gratefully. 'Though I know she means to live in Spain now, which makes things easier all round.'

'She will visit here whenever she wishes,' Cesare ordained. 'Starting with our wedding. Which—' he glanced at her speakingly, his eyes going to the slight swell where their child was growing '—I would ask to be as soon as possible.'

She looked at him, her eyes glowing with love. 'I would marry you tonight! You need only send for your chaplain!'

His hand stilled on the handle of the door before he opened it. 'Before, you wanted a civil ceremony only.'

Carla shook her head vigorously. 'Cesare—now I will marry you in your chapel here—before

God and all your ancestors. I want our marriage to last all our lives and for all eternity, for that is how long I will love you!'

She leaned into him, resting her head against his shoulder, feeling his strength, his presence, his love for her. Her hand entwined with his, the gold of his signet ring indenting her finger, their hands meshing fast, indissoluble. She felt his hand tighten in return, heard the husk in his voice as he answered her.

'And it is how long I will love *you*,' he promised her.

He took a breath, resolution in his stance as he opened their bedroom door. Beyond was the wide landing, the marble staircase sweeping down to the hall, and waiting there, he knew, would be all his household. Beyond he could see the salon doors thrown wide open, brilliantly lit, and champagne awaiting them all.

He stepped out with Carla, leading her to the head of the stairs. And as they paused for a moment, looking down, applause broke out below. He turned to Carla, raised her hand to his lips, then smiled at her, with a smile as warm as the love in his heart.

'Ready?' he murmured.

'Quite, quite ready,' she answered.

And at his side—as she would always be now—she went down with him to take her place as the woman he would marry, the woman he would love all his life—his wife and his own true love. One and the same.

The metre-thick stone walls of the castello's *chapel seemed to absorb all the low murmurings of the small, select congregation, which stilled as the priest—Cesare's chaplain—raised his hands and began to speak the words of the age-old sacrament.*

Inside her breast Carla could feel her heart beating strongly. Emotion filled her—and she felt a low, fine tremble go through her as she stood there, her cream lace gown moulding to the fullness of her ripening figure. Stood beside the man who was her bridegroom. Waiting for him to say the words that would unite them in marriage—as they were already united in love, each for each other, and both of them for the child who would soon be born to them, who would continue the ancient family of which she was now an indissoluble part.

* * * * *

LET'S TALK

For exclusive extracts, competitions
and special offers, find us online:

f facebook.com/millsandboon

⊙ @millsandboonuk

🐦 @millsandboon

Or get in touch on 0844 844 1351*

For all the latest titles coming soon,
visit millsandboon.co.uk/nextmonth

*Calls cost 7p per minute plus your phone company's price per
minute access charge

Want even more
ROMANCE?

Join our bookclub today!

**Visit millsandbook.co.uk/Bookclub
and save on brand new books.**

MILLS & BOON